Company, Ill Seen Ill Said a n d *Worstward Ho* are Samuel Beckett's late trilogy of short texts, written between 1980 and 1983. Densely poetic, they comprise some of Beckett's most radical and uncompromising works, but also among his most lyrical and heartfelt.

The Passion of D.H. Lawrence
by Jeremy Mark Robinson

Samuel Beckett Goes Into the Silence
by Jeremy Mark Robinson

Andre Gide: Fiction and Fervour in the Novels
by Jeremy Mark Robinson

The Ecstasies of John Cowper Powys
by A.P. Seabright

Amorous Life: John Cowper Powys and the Manifestation of Affectivity
by H.W. Fawkner

Postmodern Powys: New Essays on John Cowper Powys
by Joe Boulter

Rethinking Powys: Critical Essays on John Cowper Powys
edited by Jeremy Mark Robinson

Thomas Hardy and John Cowper Powys: Wessex Revisited
by Jeremy Mark Robinson

Thomas Hardy: The Tragic Novels
by Tom Spenser

Julia Kristeva: Art, Love, Melancholy, Philosophy, Semiotics
by Kelly Ives

Luce Irigaray: Lips, Kissing, and the Politics of Sexual Difference
by Kelly Ives

Helene Cixous I Love You: The Jouissance of Writing
by Kelly Ives

Emily Dickinson: Selected Poems
selected and introduced by Miriam Chalk

Petrarch, Dante and the Troubadours: The Religion of Love and Poetry
by Cassidy Hughes

Dante: *Selections From the Vita Nuova*
translated by Thomas Okey

Friedrich Holderlin: *Selected Poems*
translated by Michael Hamburger

Rainer Maria Rilke: *Selected Poems*
translated by Michael Hamburger

In the Dim Void

Samuel Beckett's Late Trilogy
Company, Ill Seen, Ill Said and *Worstward Ho*

Gregory Johns

Crescent Moon

CRESCENT MOON PUBLISHING
P.O. Box 393
Maidstone
Kent, ME14 5XU
United Kingdom

First published 1993. Second edition 2007. Fourth edition 2010.
© Gregory Johns 1993, 2007, 2010.

Printed and bound in the U.S.A.
Set in Garamond 10 on 13pt.
Designed by Radiance Graphics.

British Library Cataloguing in Publication data

Johns, Gregory
In the Dim Void: Samuel Beckett's Late Trilogy –
"Company", "Ill Seen, Ill Said" and "Worstward Ho"
1. Beckett, Samuel, 1906-1989, Company 2. Ill Seen, Ill Said
3. Worstward Ho
I. Title
843.912

ISBN-13 9781861712974

Contents

Note on Texts

English texts of the late trilogy, *Company, Ill Seen Ill Said* and *Worstward Ho,* have been used. There are many problems considering Beckett's French and English, and the relationships between them are complex. However, it is the English texts that are studied here.

Quotations from *Company* are taken from *Nohow On* (Calder, 1992)

Quotations from *Ill Seen Ill said* are taken from the British edition (Calder, 1982)

Quotations from *Worstward Ho* are taken from the British edition (Calder, 1983)

Some photos are © John Haynes. And © BBC.

Thanks to Geraldine Snowball.

Abbreviations

Collected Shorter Prose 1945-1980	Prose
Collected Poems: 1930-1978	Poems
The Complete Dramatic Works	Works
Waiting For Godot	WG
Disjecta: Miscellaneous Writings	D
The Beckett Trilogy: Molloy, Malone Dies, *The Unnamable*	T
Mercier and Camier	MC
Murphy	Mur
The Expelled and Other Novellas	E
How It Is	How
More Pricks Than Kicks	Kicks
Watt	W
Proust and Three Dialogues	Proust
Company	C
Ill Seen Ill Said	Ill
Worstward Ho	WHo
Nohow On	No
As the Story Was Told	Story
Conversations With and About Beckett	MG

Samuel Beckett

Samuel Beckett in 1963

Billie Whitelaw in Footfalls in 1976
(© John Haynes)

1

Into the Darkness

Company

We begin our voyage through Samuel Beckett's late trilogy, *Company* (1980), *Ill Seen Ill Said* (1981) and *Worstward Ho* (1983), by entering into the darkness. What darkness? The darkness at the beginning of *Company*:

> A voice comes to one in the dark. Imagine.

> To one on his back in the dark. This he can tell by the pressure on his hind parts and by how the dark changes when he shuts his eyes and again when he opens them again. (No, 5)

This is where we begin.

In the darkness. On our back in the darkness. This is a typical Beckettian stance, this recumbent experience: so many Beckett protagonists lie down and reflect. For this state, this text. is primarily reflective. It induces contemplation, memories, self-reflexivity.

Again and again the narrator of the text reminds 'him' that 'he is on his back in the dark'. In the dark in a room. Any room. A womb, even.

Automatically, then, we are in memory-mode here, and this is our primary position: to lie on our back in the dark.

Samuel Beckett speaks of

needing to 'sink down' into 'the darkness' before he writes. That is, to get into the right mood, and then to sink down into it.[1] Always in Beckett's work we find this vertical motion, this sinking downwards. It is 'vertical meditation', as the Zen Buddhists call it. In the Christian mystical tradition Meister Eckhart spoke of needing to sink down 'from nothingness to nothingness'.

So this state, of lying in the dark, is a meditative state, seemingly 'passive', in that it allows memories, feelings, ideas and experiences to wash over the protagonist. Psychologically, the person is allowing the unconscious to swallow them up. And, lo and behold, in this darkness a voice speaks. We find this scenario – of someone on screen, on stage or in a space, listening to a dis-embodied voice – through-out Beckett's work. In *Eb, Joe*, in the *Texts For Nothing*, in *The Unnamable*, in *Footfalls*.

In that first sentence of

Samuel Beckett's trilogy we have the archetypal Beckettian scenario, of one listening to another in the dark. The spacelessness of it all indicates psychic processes at work: superego talking to ego, conscience talking to self, shadow confronting the self, projections upon projections, minds within minds, people creating voices which create people. It's often a case of Chinese boxes with Beckett. Texts within texts, memories within memories, lives within lives.

Already, in that first sequence, we have an evoc-ation of darkness, voices, truth, memory, black/ white, and death. The narrator is not sure of it all. Not only do we have darkness and someone lying on their back and a voice talking to them, we also have uncertainty and ambiguity: '[o]nly a small part of what is said can be verified' (No, 5). After this statement, by the omniscient narrator speaking of the voice speaking in the dark to the character in the room, we have the classic Beckett

---

1 Beckett wrote in longhand, he said, then typed up his work.

evocation: of darkness and light, of light amidst darkness:

> But by far the greater part of what is said cannot be verified. As for example when he hears, You first saw the light on such and such a day. Sometimes the two combined as for example, You first saw the light on such and such a day and now you are on your back in the dark. (No, 5)

From then on the 1980-83 trilogy is a mass of Beckettian oppositions and dualities, which are also the archetypal ones of all Western art:

> darkness/ light,
> fear/ desire,
> male/ female,
> present/ past,
> speaking and creating/
> silence and uncreation,
> less/ more,
> distance/ closeness,
> presence/ absence,
> solitude/ company,
> love/ hate,
> everything/ nothing,
> imagination/ death

These are the basic oppositions in Samuel Beckett's work, often symbolized by light and dark, visually, or embodied in two people, physically, who argue, dialectically. Beckett veers from one extreme to another, and loves dialogue and dialectic. Statements are immediately countered. Nothing is fixed. All is flux, as Heraclitus said. Taking their cue from Socrates and Georg Wilhelm Friedrich Hegel, Beckett's protagonists argue like mad – even more than William Shakespeare's clowns. In so many of Beckett's works we find two people pitted against each other: in *Mercier and Camier, Waiting for Godot, Endgame.*

> VLADIMIR: It's always at nightfall.
> ESTRAGON: But night doesn't fall.
> VLADIMIR: It'll fall all of a sudden, like yesterday.
> ESTRAGON: Then it'll be night.
> VLADIMIR: And we can go.
> ESTRAGON: Then it'll be day again. (*Pause. Despairing.*) What'll we do, what'll we do![2]

Sam Beckett will not keep

---

2 *Waiting For Godot*, 46.

19

still – either linguistically, philosophically, psychologically or ideologically.[3] He enjoys changing things, continually. He enjoys changing a word and watching the critics go mad trying to accommodate the new change. Thus, he changes things when he moves from the French to the English version of a text. He changes things when he directs plays. He is always changing himself, and his texts reflect these changes. *Waiting for Godot*, for instance, the central play of 20th century drama, has been changed by the author (in Berlin in 1975, for instance, and the 1984 San Quentin Drama workshop

production.)[4]

This artistic sense of flux applies directly to the late *Company* trilogy, which appeared in French and English. Brian Fitch states that the French and English texts of *Company* are not simply translations, but two different texts. It is not a question, with Beckett, of translating as closely as possible from one language to another. No. Beckett changes many levels of his texts in translation, so that *Company* and *Compagnie* are not the same texts. Brian Fitch writes:

neither version can be appropriately substituted

---

3 For Beckett research on the internet, there is a welter of websites. Good ones to start with are the Samuel Beckett Society (ua.ac.be), samuel-beckett.com, samuel-beckett.net, samuelbeckett.it and themodernword.com. There's also the journals *Samuel Beckett Today* and *Journal of Beckett Studies.*

4 See Colin Duckworth: "Beckett 's New Godot", in James Ascheson, 175-192; Ruby Cohn, 1980; and the staging of *Company* is discussed in S.E. Gontarski: "*Company* for Company: Androgyny and Theatricality in Samuel Beckett's Prose", in J. Ascheson, 193-202. Lori Chamberlain says both the French and English texts are 'secondary' (in "The Same Old Stories": Beckett's Poetics of Translation", in Friedman, 17f). And Marjorie Perloff writes: 'The scene of Beckett's writing exists somewhere in between the two, a space where neither French nor English has autonomy.' ("Une Voix pas la mienne: French/ English Beckett and the French/ English", in Friedman, 47)

for the other by the critic: each has to be studied in its own right, together with the precise relationship existing between the two.[5]

So *Company, Ill Seen Ill Said* and *Worstward Ho* are texts that are in motion. This is how Samuel Beckett likes it. For his texts themselves continually contradict each other, within their labyrinthine interiors. Thus, as soon as one thing is said, the opposite quickly counters it. In *Company* we see this push-me-pull-you dialectic going on all through the text.

Samuel Beckett is wary of direct statements. They cannot be true, he feels. Statements must not be didactic, they must be delivered with irony and humour, with a knowing-ness, a self-awareness. Yet, at the same time, Beckett yearns for absolute authority, for a statement that unflinchingly says something. Thus, in *Company*, the narrator tells the 'one on his back in the dark' that he hears a voice, but the voice or the narrator admits ambiguity and uncertainty: '[o]nly a small part of what is said can be verified' (7).

And this is the whole problem, the whole tension, at the the heart of the late *Nohow* trilogy, and at the heart of Beckett's work, this uncertainty which infuses every level of experience of Beckett's world. While Hamlet might have wondered whether 'to be or not to be' was the key question, Beckett wonders whether one can even conceive let alone speak such a question.

The tension in Samuel Beckett's works revolves around speaking/ not speaking, which is a linguistic form of the basic Existential, ontological exploration in his work. To speak is to perhaps make again the connection with other voices. This is the search for 'company' at the heart of *Company*: '[t]he need to hear that voice again' (45)

The emotional core of *Company* is a nostalgic yearning, manifested in those vignettes or memories, which

---

5 Brian T. Fitch, in A. Friedman, 25

some see as having correlations with Beckett's own life, so that *Company* is the closest thing in the Beckett canon to autobiography.6

Certainly many of the sections in *Company* have the whiff of autobiography, but these are memories mediated, edited, shaped, compressed and transformed by Samuel Beckett's various voices. For in *Company* we find a narrator, a voice, a remembering self, in fact a complex hierarchy of various levels of consciousness and self-consciousness. Some of the passages are Beckett at his most lyrical, his most self-indulgently lyrical, one might add, for no sooner is lyricism evoked than it is stamped out. Ornamental writing is detested by Beckett, yet he can be as poetic in the ecstatic sense as any other poet. Here is a powerful sequence from *Company*:

---

6 See Linda Ben-Zvi: "Fritz Mauthner for 'Company'", *Journal of Beckett Studies* (9), 1984, 76; Brian Finney: "*Still* to *Worstward Ho*: Beckett's Prose Fiction Since *The Lost Ones*", in J. Ascheson, 69; Mary A. Doll: "Walking and rocking: ritual Acts in *Footfalls* and *Rockaby*", in R. Davies, 53

the light there was then. On your back in the dark the light there was then. Sunless cloudless brightness. You slip away at break of day and climb to your hiding place on the hillside. A nook in the gorse. East beyond the sea the faint shape of high mountain. Seventy miles away according to your Longman. For the third or fourth time in your life. The first time you told them and were derided. All you had seen was clod. So now you heard it in your heart with the rest. Back home at nightfall supperless to bed. You lie in the dark and are back in that light. Straining out from your nest in the gorse with your eyes across the water until they ache. You close them while you count a hundred. Then open and strain again. Again and again. Till in the end it is there. Palest blue against the pale sky. You lie in the dark and are back in that light. Fall asleep in that sunless cloudless light. Sleep till morning light. (20)

This memory sequence is a kind of ecstasy. An everyday sort of ecstasy, perhaps, but even Beckett's rigorous control of language and his hyper-realist outlook on life cannot hide the joy in this passage. For there *is* joy in Beckett's art, though always, as in Thomas Hardy's fiction, very brief joy, soon smothered by all manner of other concerns.

Light accompanies most Beckettian ecstasies. Samuel Beckett is always very concerned with light. There is the gradually dimming light in *Footfalls* and *Rockaby*, the two plays which, with *Not I*, form an alternative late trilogy (and might also be called the Billie Whitelaw trilogy, for the amazing actress is the heart of the trilogy of plays. Whitelaw performing Beckett's drama in London in 1986 was about the best thing I've ever seen in the theatre. An absolutely spellbinding performance, so breathtaking you literally held your breath in astonishment the whole time).

Light out of darkness is a predominant theme in Beckett's art. Light is undoubtedly creative. It relates to the creative act of God, *let there be light*. In Beckett's poetic world, the dictum is: *let the light fade to black*.

There are many kinds of darkness in Beckett's writing and many kinds of lightness. As in *Company* he writes: '[t]he test is company. Which of the two darks is the better company.' (21) For light-in-darkness is surely a kind of company; the light coming is analogous in Beckett's world to speaking. The light comes on and the voice begins, as in the plays, where the light shines on a performer, and they speak.

The two, light and voice, are bound up together in Samuel Beckett's work to form a poetry of post-Symbolist synæsthesia, where, as in Arthur Rimbaud's poesie, vowels have colours and the musicality of words became a concrete, plastic thing.

For no Samuel Beckett text comprises of total blackness and total silence. Oh no, that would be going too far. Beckett is not apocalyptic; he does not want to get rid of *every*thing and *every*body. No. He retains light fading up out of darkness, and just a little voice in the silence.

Light helps, as does speaking. To have light brightening in darkness enlivens things a little, as does hearing a voice in the silence. This is the meaning of 'company' in *Company*:

> What visions in the dark of light! Who exclaims thus? Who asks who exclaims? What visions in the shadeless dark of light and shade! Yet another still? Devising it all for company. What a further addition to company that would be! Yet another still devising it all for company. (49)

It is the writer who 'devises it all for company'. The artist makes her own world in her art. Then she goes and lives in it. So too does Beckett the author create his worlds, and then he lives in them. Beckett's worlds are devised for his own satisfaction. All artists do this. Where would Francesco Petrarch love to be

but in the sophisticated lyrical world of his *Rime Sparse*, where poets languish beside the pure waters of the Vaucluse fountain and dream of Laura the beloved? Where would J.R.R. Tolkien rather be than wandering around Middle-earth, speaking Elvish with Elves and eating breakfast with hobbits?

Samuel Beckett knows that writers live in the worlds they create. Yet Beckett's worlds are not wholly naturalistic. True, the landscapes of *More Pricks Than Kicks, Waiting for Godot, Endgame, Molloy* and *Texts For Nothing* are well defined. But they are simultaneously literary landscapes, landscapes of the mind and soul. They are symbolic, nostalgic, psychic. They have more to do with mental processes than real places. Thus, in *Company*, each landscape - of the shops, the hills, the home - are mediated by memory, then channelled through the writing processes, which in Beckett's output are particularly complex.

The light in *Company*,

then, is a psychological, even religious, light. No matter what he can do, Beckett's narrators can never quite shake off their vision of the light. Once upon a time they saw the light. There's no point denying it. They saw the light. They experienced pure light. And we find this again and again in Beckett's work.

In *Company*, the light refers to 'first seeing the light', that is, being born. But it also refers to the brilliance of the sky, to the glow that adults throw around childhood, to the spaces of youth. For the light, in *Company* at least, is positive and enriching. It is not the harsh white light of *Ping* or *All Strange Away*. It is, rather, a light that is at times unmistakably religious. The light comes and it is like an Act of God. It is equated with the Voice of God, of some divine creator. Not explicitly, but implicitly:

> By the voice a faint light is shed. Dark lightens while it sounds. Deepens when it ebbs. Lightens with flow back to faint full. Is whole

again when it ceases. You are on your back in the dark. Had the eyes been open then they would have marked a change. Whence the shadowy light? What company in the dark! To close the eyes and try to imagine that. Whence once the shadowy light. No source. As if faintly luminous all his little void. (15)

In each of the nostalgic sequences in *Company* light features prominently, as in the snowlit scene, a classic Beckettian reminiscence, where the narrator notes that peculiar lightning which snow beings: lighting from below ('[t]he dark scene seems lit from below.'):

> To be gone. Then the snowlit scene. You lie in the dark with closed eyes and see yourself there as described making ready to strike out and away across the expanse of light. (28)

Light in religion is a mark of the primary manifestation of the divine. The very word for God or a deity, *deus*,

25

means 'shining one'.7 In Beckett's work, there are many 'shining ones'. In the late *Company* trilogy, a major 'shining one', Venus, appears early on in *Ill Seen Ill Said* as a key element in the text.

Throughout Samuel Beckett's work, the religious dimension of light is suppressed but never wholly obliterated. Beckett is a very self-aware writer, and he knows when he is being allusive. The final paragraph of *Ill Seen Ill Said*, for instance, alludes, according to Marjorie Perloff, to John Keats and Gerald Manley Hopkins.8 So when Beckett writes about light, he knows about the mystical meanings of it.

It is typical that in Beckett's poetic world the light in memories should be brighter and more important than the light in the present. Memories are brighter, because they are bathed in nostalgia. Thus, people look back on childhood as a happy time when the summers were hotter and better than the ones now, even if facts state they are the same. Paradise is a powerful myth, and the 'green world' of childhood is no myth, either, it is a psychological reality.

It is this early paradisal realm of childhood that suffuses *Company*, and much of Samuel Beckett's other fictions and dramas. So many Beckett protagonists look back on the past with fondness, as well as contempt. Thus, Krapp thinks back to being in the boat, while May in *Footfalls* goes back over the past too. Beckett's people cannot leave the past alone. When they are alone, their thoughts are the only things they have for company. Beckett's selfs alone are thrown back on their own emotional resources. They think, they dream, they muse. They are alone, they are in the dark, so

7 See Weston La Barre: *Muelos*, p 80: 'the Indo-European **diew...* means literally only "the shining one"... It can refer to the sun (or moon), the sky, the divine planets, lightning, Soma, light, life, and fire, as simply manifestations of the same phenomenon: the divine light.'

8 Marjorie Perloff, op.cit., in Friedman, 43

they start to remember. They cannot help remembering, like Marcel Proust's protagonists.

Light becomes a way in to mnemonic exercises. The particular quality of certain lights is a way in to the past. Thus, the narrator of *Company* recalls the particular '[s]unless cloudless brightness' up there on the hillside (19). That is very particular kind of lighting, that sunless and cloudless brightness. And always in Beckett's art the *type* of lighting – its direction, pattern, hue, intensity and field – is crucial. Beckett always makes sure we have a clear idea of the lightning. In *Footfalls*, for instance, the lighting defined the emotional space of the piece. Beckett's sense of drama is about space and stasis. Keir Elam writes that 'the text is defined and perceived above all in spatial terms.'[9]

Out with his mother, the rememberer in *Company* thinks back to the skies of his childhood. He pictures the scene clearly:

> You make ground in silence hand in hand through the warm still summer air. It is late afternoon and after some hundred paces the sun appears above the crest of the rise. Looking up at the blue sky and then at your mother's face you break the silence asking her if it is not in reality much more distant than it appears. The sky that is. The blue sky. (8)

Gods live in the sky, and since time immemorial the sky has been regarded as something sacred, as a manifestation of the sacred. It is where the gods live, where the stars and planets revolve, influencing our lives, where aliens come from in sci-fi, where heaven is, etc. As Mircea Eliade writes:

> I believe, personally, that it is through consideration of the sky's immensity that man is led to a revelation of transcendence, of the sacred.[10]

9 Keir Elam: *The Semiotics of Theatre and Drama*, Methuen 1980, 56

10 Mircea Eliade, 1984, 162

In Samuel Beckett's work we find much preoccupation with skies, with Dantean celestial realms, with astrology (in the early poem 'Whoroscope', for example). *Ill Seen Ill Said*, in particular, is concerned with magical rites to do with the rising and setting of stars, of the 'zone of stones', of coming and going (= living and dying).

Understandably in a poet of self-conscious, studied melancholy, Samuel Beckett employs twilight a lot (as does another hyper self-aware writer, André Gide, who in *Paludes* produced a very Beckettian text, while Gide's *The Counterfeiters* investigates language and the relation of the author to her/his work with as much vigour as Beckett's *The Unnamable*). What modern poet, indeed, has not written evocatively of twilight – from T.S. Eliot to Rainer Maria Rilke, from Arthur Rimbaud to C.P. Cavafy. Twilight, from Johann Wolfgang von Goethe and John Keats onwards, is a prerequisite of modern poetry. 'This evening, it's always evening, always spoken of as evening, even when it's morning', as the narrator notes in the fifth of the *Texts For Nothing* (Prose, 87).

In *Company* twilight appears in the memory sequences, while in *Ill Seen Ill Said* it seems to be perpetually sunrise or sundown. In *Company* we find this archetypal piece of Beckett in his lyrical mode:

A strand. Evening. Light dying. Soon none left to die. No. No such thing then as no light. Died on to dawn and never died. You stand with you back to the wash. No sound but its. Ever fainter as it slowly ebbs. Till it slowly flows again. You lean on a long staff. Your hands rest on the knob and on them your head. Were your eyes to open they would first see far below in the last rays the skirt of your greatcoat and the uppers of your boots emerging from the sand. Then and it alone till it vanishes the shadow of the staff on the sand. Vanishes from your sight. Moonless starless night. Were your eyes to open dark would lighten. (44)

The '[m]oonless starless night' is a symbol of purity, like the '[s]unless cloudless brightness'.[11] Each light is pure, swept clean of allusions, complications and tensions. One imagines that Beckett was aiming in this late *Nohow* trilogy for a prose or a text that was pure, as the sky is sometimes pure, as the sky of childhood, in memory, is sometimes pure, purely cloudless, sunless, moonless and starless (Beckett's plentiful use of the word endings 'ness' and 'less' is oddly compelling. Only Beckett would consider employing terms like 'lessness' so often, and making them work).

There is a deep yearning in Samuel Beckett's fictions for a pure means of expression, a 'literature of the unword' as he called it,[12] a literature purged of everything except the essence itself. This is a dream found in the work of Stendhal, in Gustave Flaubert, in Stéphane Mallarmé and in André Gide. It is a dream of a transparent form of expression, of a poetics reduced to its bare bones. We see Beckett searching for this kind of poetics throughout his writing career, from the relentless reductionism of *The Unnamable* to the increasingly sparse texts of the 1960s, and finally to the late 1980-83 trilogy, which, from *Company* to *Worstward Ho,* becomes ever more reduced to the bare essentials of communication, to sentences often without verbs, to a state of nouns, which, as Gertrude Stein noted, was one of the functions of poetry, that is, to always 'deal with the

---

11 While talking about Sam Beckett and symbolism, we should remember Jack McGowran's remark that 'there are many avenues of approach, ways of looking at things. The first avenue is the simple thread. It can't be that, but with Beckett it is, as it is with all great writers. He said, 'People read great symbolism I never intended.'' (MG, 22).

---

12 In a letter of 1937, in *Disjecta*, 173

noun'.[13]

The central reminiscence of *Company*, and indeed one of the most passionately lyrical in all Beckett's art, is the two lovers sitting in the summerhouse. This is undiluted eroticism, seen through the rose-tinted glasses of nostalgia, which are deliberately echoed in the rosy coloured panes of glass in the summerhouse building. The memory begins with an evocation of the pure kind of day which is the landscape of each memory sequence in *Company*:

> Bloom of adulthood. Imagine a whiff of that. On your back in the dark you remember. Ah you you remember. Cloudless May day. She joins you in the summerhouse.(31)

A description, so typical of Samuel Beckett, follows of the summerhouse numbers, dimensions, precise spatial delineations. Extraordinarily in Beckett's art, this nostalgic review of youth is characterized by nothing less than 'rainbow light':

> You press your little nose against the pane and all without is rosy. The years have flown and there at the same as then you sit in the bloom of adulthood bathed in rainbow light gazing before you. (32)

Present and past commingle as the remembering voice flits from there to here, from then to now, from past to present. The irony is, as ever, that the past seems more 'real', more poignant, more acute and alive than the present. This is the problem of many a poet, from Francesco Petrarch through Robert Herrick to Robert Graves. The past was wonderful because at least you were really alive then. Now you are simply alone in the dark, remembering, hardly alive at all. Yet, alive at least a little, because these memories themselves are a

---

13 See Gertrude Stein: *Look at me and here I am: Writings and Lectures, 1911-45*, ed. Patricia Meyerowitz, Peter Owen 1967, 136: 'Poetry is concerned with using with abusing, with losing with wanting, with denying with avoiding with adoring with replacing the noun. It is doing that always doing that, doing that and doing nothing but that. Poetry is doing nothing but using losing refusing and pleasing and betraying and caressing nouns.'

kind of company, a kind of solace.

Further precise spatial descriptions follow, of the bodies in the summerhouse. But even these pieces of geometry and mathematics cannot mask the deep lyricism and eroticism of the memory:

> How given you were both moving and at rest to the closed eye in your waking hours! by day and by night. To that perfect dark. That shadowless light. Simply to be gone... So you sit face to face in the little summer-house. With eyes closed and your hands on your pubes. In that rainbow light. That dead still.

The scene – sitting motionless in some glowing light – is a key motif in late Samuel Beckett, from *Still* onwards. So many of Beckett's protagonists simply sit and gaze. Nothing 'happens', in the usual sense of the word. There is no 'action', there is simply sitting and *being*.

The motionless pose in the summerhouse recalls so many of Beckett's earlier texts, those short fizzles and pings, such as *Lessness, Closed Space, Ping* and *Imagination Dead Imagine.* This static posture, used to such great effect in *Rockaby*, is the endpoint of the earlier Beckettian struggles through the undergrowth, along hillsides and through the back streets of towns. Now the Beckettian protagonists, in these late works, echo precisely the posture of the writer, sitting at her table, creating. The writer sits still and writes, and the character does too. The writer writes, but the Beckett character gazes. Beckett's characters sitting still and musing while the light fades emulate precisely the writer at her table writing while the sky darkens. This scenario is at its most exquisite in *Still*, which is a superbly poetic text, and the most tranquil in all Beckett's *œuvre*:

> Bright at last close of a dark day the sun shines out at last and goes down. Sitting quite still at valley window normally turn head now and see it the

sun low in the southwest
sinking. Even get up
certain moods and go
stand by western window
quite still watching it sink
and then the afterglow.
Always quite still some
reason some time past
this hour at open window
facing south in small
upright wicker chair with
armrests. Eyes stare out
unseeing till first
movement some time past
close though unseeing
still while still light.
(Prose, 183)

2

What When Words Gone?

Beckett and Language

Still focuses wholly on language and expression. Text becomes primary, and the text is the story. All of Samuel Beckett's texts are meta-texts, texts about texts, texts within texts, texts describing other texts, texts that are acutely aware of themselves as texts, texts *qua* texts, as Beckett might put it. But in the late works, from the short fictions of the 1960s onwards, from *All Strange Away* and *Enough* onwards, the texts became wholly concerned with themselves, and how they mirror, parody and feed off other texts, usually the author's own pieces. What occurs is a cluster of texts that are deeply interrelated, not only with each other, but with their French and English versions, so that Beckett's post-*Godot* works are mirrors within mirrors, a web of signifieds, yet Beckett's meticulous grasp of lingual expression confers a unity of the texts.

In the later works Samuel Beckett's dictum that 'form is content, content is form'[14] becomes the basis for artistic endeavour. Each text makes form primary. Surfaces are

---

14 In "Dante… Bruno.Vico… Joyce", in *Disjecta*, 27

everything. It is not a question of 'all surface and no depth', for Beckett's surfaces are very deep.

Words have always been primary for Samuel Beckett. Like James Joyce, like William Shakespeare, like Dante Aligheri, Beckett loves words. Yet, like the post-Symbolist writers, such as Paul Valéry, Beckett knows the limitations of words. He knows that words can only go so far. This is one of his main struggles, with language, meaning and syntax. As T.S. Eliot said, writing poetry is working with limitations.

Ludwig Wittgenstein and Karl Kraus wrote lucidly of the limits of language. Wittgenstein's philosophy has affinities with Beckett's radical writing. For Wittgenstein, the limits of language are the limits of his world. In his *Tractatus Logico-Philosophicus*, Wittgenstein wrote:

> The world is *my* world; this is manifest in the fact that the limits of *language*... mean the limits of *my* world.[15]

The central paradox in Samuel Beckett's art is the tension between the passionate desire to speak and the passionate desire for not speaking. All through Beckett's career we find the tensions between speaking and silence worked out in all manner of ways. In his *Dialogues* Beckett explains his thesis:

> B. – The situation is that of him who is helpless, cannot act, in the event cannot paint, since he is obliged to paint. The act is of him who, helpless, unable to act, acts, in the event paints, since he is obliged to paint.
> D. – Why is he obliged to paint?
> B. – I don't know.
> D. – Why is he helpless to paint?
> B. – Because there is nothing to paint and nothing to paint with. (D, 142)

This is the problem of all Samuel Beckett's anti-heroes: to speak without having

---

15 L. Wittgenstein: *Tractatus Logico-Philosophicus*, 1961

anything to say; to write without having the means. And it is the problem of the narrators, who relate the texts within which Beckett's protagonists shuffle and sit, and it is the problem of the author, the one who sets in motion the whole fiasco.

Again, in *Dialogues*, Beckett says:

> The expression that there is nothing to express, nothing with which to express, nothing from which to express, no power to express, no desire to express, together with the obligation to express. (D, 139)

Samuel Beckett's anti-heroes 'go on', and Beckett the writer 'goes on'. He never quite stops writing, though he dreams of stopping writing. To bring an end to it is a deep desire in Beckett's *œuvre*. 'Farewell to farewell,' as he puts it at the end of *Ill Seen Ill Said*, 'the whole kit and boodle' (59). Vladimir and Estragon yearn to put an end to it. To what? To 'it all', as May says in *Footfalls*, 'it all' meaning the whole thing, all of life. Yet they always go on, Beckett's people always go on. As the self in *The Unnamable* says 'but unconditionally, I resume' (T, 367).

To be silent is to be, but to speak is a livelier kind of being. Samuel Beckett's characters love silence more than speech, but they keep speaking. You can't print a book of silence, of blank pages. Or you can, but only once. After that, no one would buy it. John Cage might produce three minutes of silence, but, again, this is a one-off thing. Although there are different kinds of silence (the silence of a room in the country by night is quite different from the momentary silence in a town when the traffic stops roaring when the lights are on red), in a book, using words, only a certain kind of silence can be created.

What Beckett does is to gradually prune away the excess, until there is nothing left but the bare essentials. In fact, it is in the spaces between his words that we must look for his true meaning. Cultural theorists state

35

that ideology is what is between the words in a text, what is there embedded in a text, what is obvious as well as what is hidden. Terry Eagleton writes: '[i]t is in the significant *silences* of a text, in its gaps and absences that the presence of ideology can be most positively felt.'[16]

What Samuel Beckett does is to cultivate a poetics of absence, where the silence is present in the spaces between words, where the meaning resides in *what is not said*, rather than in what is said. What Beckett leaves out of his texts is as crucial as what he puts in. Thus, his texts are supremely *meta-texts*, for they are freighted with masses of invisible material, rather like the universe is composed of 'dark matter', the stuff we cannot see but which makes up a large part of the stuff of the universe.

In Samuel Beckett's work, the real meaning is in the 'dark matter' of the texts, in the gaps, which are often vast gulfs, between word and meaning, between word and word, in Beckett's 'literature of the unword', as he puts it.

Samuel Beckett's sense of poetry is a poetics of 'un-writing'. He loves to express things in negatives. Thus he speaks of having 'nothing to express'. Much as in *Alice in Wonderland* there is talk of 'undancing' or 'undoing', of doing things backwards, of having 'unbirthdays'. Like Lewis Carroll, Beckett happily celebrates 'unbirthdays' rather than birthdays. Similarly, his texts are very much 'untexts'. They are the 'un-writings' of someone who is by default an 'un-writer'.

The whole of Beckett's poetic career is a movement towards 'un-writing', towards a 'literature of the unword'. In piece after piece, Beckett strips his texts down. It's an exciting process to watch. After all, the ending of *The Unnamable* seemed quite severe, but Beckett went much further with *How It Is*. Then we had the reduced short texts of the 1960s, and in *Ping* and *Lessness* it seemed Beckett had got to the

---

16 Terry Eagleton: *Marxism and Literary Criticism*, University of California Press, Berkeley 1976, 34

end of his linguistic reductionism. But no. Along came the late trilogy, *Company, Ill See Ill Said* and *Worstward Ho.*

Company is still largely a recognizable novelistic format, with its person/ self in the dark remembering its life. But the other two are distinctly disintegrated texts, meta-texts, texts about/ within/ around texts. The usual narrative structures have been disregarded. A new kind of text emerges.

Still Samuel Beckett wields images, however. Still he cannot wrench himself free of conjuring up pictures with his prose. It's the *jouissance* of writing, the joy of creating metaphors, images, dramas.

Thus, in *Ill Seen Ill Said* we have a very clear picture of the old woman and the 'zone of stones'. In these late works, which seem so difficult to grasp, Beckett still furnishes us with mathematical measurements! We could plot out the stone circle or the summerhouse on the ground if we wished. We could build the spaces of each text, if we wished. However vague he might be in other areas, Beckett always makes sure the reader has an acute sense of space and environment.

The complex web of speaking, voices, listeners/ readers and meanings is at the heart of *Company, Ill Seen Ill Said* and *Worstward Ho.* There is a very definite fear of words stopping, of there being no voice speaking. This is death for Beckett, the end of the voice. It means total obliteration, utter oblivion. Not to speak is hell for him. He must always speak. As the narrator of *Worstward Ho* puts it:

> What when words gone?
> None for what then...
> What words for what
> then? None for what then.
> No words for what when
> words gone. For what
> when nohow on.
> Somehow nohow on. (28)

The situation when 'words [have] gone' is terrifying to a writer such as Sam Beckett, who exalts words, who worships words even as he despises them. A wordless world is an impossibility for him – or for his narrators. Yet, somehow, things go on, even without words, even when everything is dimmed in the dim void to almost nothingness:

> Somehow nohow on. (28)

This is what happens: the voice, the narrator, the self speaking the voice, somehow – nohow – goes on.

The obsession with words, with the power of The Word, is found in Beckett's 'final literary utterance',[17] *What is the Word*:

> folly seeing all this
> this –
> what is the word –
> this this –
> this this here –
> …what –
> what is the word –
>
> what is the word –
> (Story, 132-4)

What's clear about *Company* is that is veers between a traditional text, with its evocations of images and memories, and a postmodern revision of fiction, where every step in the naturalistic evocation process is questioned. Thus, the late trilogy, beginning with *Company*, is an act of self-questioning, an exploration of the act of writing fiction. Thus, even as the narrator brings in the voice to the one in the dark, questions are raised. Who is the voice? Who is speaking to whom? What is the relation of the author to the narrator to the voice to the self to the one in the dark? ('For why or? why in another dark or in the same? And whose voice asking this? Who asks, Whose voice asking this?' [19]).

The voice comes to 'him' in the dark and tells him things. For Samuel Beckett, voices speaking in darkness is not simply a perfect picture of the author and his text, the author speaking through his text, it is also a very real, physical experience. For instance, of his play *Not I*, Beckett said: 'I heard "her" saying what I wrote in *Not I*. I actually heard it.'[18] And,

---

17 Preface to *As the Story Was Told*, written by 'The Publishers', 10

18 Quoted in Deirdre Bair, 622

interestingly, Beckett himself did not wish to have his own voice recorded:

> This famous voice is everywhere, but also nowhere to be heard, for Beckett refuses to allow his voice to be recorded; this refusal exists in strange, erotic complicity with the dependence on this voice of those with whom he works.[19]

These voices coming out of the darkness – to Joe in *Eh, Joe*, to May in *Footfalls*, to the one in the dark in *Company* – are actual, palpable voices, as well as psychic events (superego to ego, or unconscious speaking to the self, etc). The voices provide 'company', and to have a voice oneself, if the 'one in the dark' can have a voice, that too is 'company' of a kind: '[p]erhaps even to have a voice. To murmur, Yes I remember. What an addition to company that would be!' (12)

The voice means presence; the text can remain presenceless, but the voice means there is a speaker, a human presence. As Toril Moi explains:

> Western metaphysics comes to favour speech over writing precisely because speech pre-supposes the *presence* of the speaking subject... The idea that a text is somehow only fully *authentic* when it expresses the presence of a human subject would be one example of the implicit privileging of voice or speech over writing.[20]

The voice in Samuel Beckett's writing operates in the intermediary realm between presence and absence. There are real or imagined voices in *Company*, while in *Footfalls* the voice of the mother is the voice of someone who is (probably) dead. In his book *Deconstruction*, Christopher Norris writes of Jacques Derrida's investigation of writing and speaking, which are central to Beckett's mythopœia:

---

19 S. Connor, 192

20 Toril Moi, 1985, 107

Voice becomes a metaphor of truth and authenticity, a source of self-present 'living' speech as opposed to the secondary lifeless emanations of writing. In speaking one is able to experience (supposedly) an intimate link between sound and sense, an inward and immediate realization of meaning which yields itself up without reserve to perfect, transparent under-standing. Writing, on the contrary, destroys this ideal of pure self-presence. It obtrudes an alien, depersonalized medium, a deceiving shadow which falls between intent and meaning, between utterance and under-standing. It occupies a promiscuous public realm where authority is sacrificed to the vagaries and whims of textual 'dissemination'. Writing, in short, is a threat to the deeply traditional view that associates truth with self-presence and the 'natural' language wherein it finds expression.[21]

The voices, the words, the act of writing are all forms of 'company'. Writing is a mirror. André Gide spoke of 'writing into a mirror', for if one has no one else to write about, then one can write about the self, as so many do. Gide props up a mirror and writes into it.[22]

In Beckett's late trilogy this self-reflexivity or *mise-en-âbyme* is taken to extremes. For each book in the 1980-83 trilogy is a commentary on the text, even as the text is being written. Do it like this? Or like that? the narrator asks himself continually. Sometimes, the narrator asks a blissfully silly question, as in *Company*: '[c]an the crawling creator crawling in the same create dark as his creature create while crawling?' (43)

Thus, in *Ill Seen Ill Said* we have those little encour-agements of the narrator to himself: '[G]ently gently. On. Careful.' (20) At the beginning of *Worstward Ho* the narrator has doubts right from the beginning, and has to encourage himself with

---

21 Christopher Norris:
Deconstruction: Theory and Practice,
Methuen 1982, 28

22 See Jeremy Robinson, 1992

various words, 'on' being perhaps the most positive. Indeed, the very term 'on' is proof of Beckett's dogged optimism. He's always writing it. 'On'. It helps the author and the narrator, as much as the characters, to go on, to continue. Somehow, nohow, the show must go on. The text continues:

> On. Say on. Be said on. Somehow on. Till nohow on. Said nohow on. (WHo, 7)

The late trilogy is a rich work of multiple layers, and the author is not sure which layer he wants uppermost. He pushes forward the memories, then the commentary on the memories, then the effect of the memories on the 'one in the dark', then the voice in the dark, and so on. Each layer is as equally important as the others. Though the tension between yearning for company and the ability to do without companionship is not underlined at every stage in *Company*'s text, it is crucial to the understanding of the work.

It is all a construction, this book. It's an invention. Yet underneath the self-questioning is deep desire. Most critics acknowledge the syntactic and semantic structure of the work, such as Kateryna Arthur:

> The 'company' that the work speaks of is the accumulation of self-generated constructions in the form of inventions and memories which inhabit the world of the imagination and which, for a writer, provide the material (the Yeatsian 'rag and bone') for the world of his works.[23]

Yet too few critics acknowledge the immense pain and desire in Samuel Beckett's works. Most critics acknowledge the Existential angst in *Waiting For Godot* and *The Trilogy*, but too few recognize that that immense yearning for contact lies behind most if not all of Beckett's works. Even when he is exploring the limits of language and expression, in works such as *How It Is* and

---

23 Kateryna Arthur" "Texts for *Company*", in J. Ascheson, 136.

Worstward Ho, there is still much yearning for making contact with something supermeaningful – preferably another voice, another self, another soul.

Cultural theory and postmodern critics note in Beckett's work the exploration of self-reflexivity, self-identity, subjectivity, *mise-en-âbyme* and so on, but their emphasis on the form and structure of Beckett's texts displaces the emotional content. And the emotional or spiritual feeling in Beckett's output is crucial. Otherwise, he wouldn't bother to write. His works are not 'experiments' merely. They are not simply playing about with colours and textures. They come from the soul, really, from the heart. And while the writers Beckett admires – Dante Alighieri, James Joyce, W.B. Yeats, Johann Wolfgang von Goethe, Arthur Rimbaud – are brilliant innovators in poetics and expression, they are also deeply emotional

and spiritual creators.[24]

So when the narrator of *Company* says he is 'devising it all for company' he is not only acknowledging the precariousness of the artistic enterprise, with its many layers of meaning and authority and its hesitations, he is also acknowledging the yearning that drives the whole endeavour. At times, it seems the narrator, or the 'one in the dark', or the voice, or whoever, is '[d]evising figments to temper his nothingness' (37), but he/ it is also devising figments to provide solace in his yearning. Whoever is doing the speaking, whether it is the deviser or the '[d]evised deviser', it is all being devised for company (37).

Company ends on a note of resignation, resignation to the facts of life: that we are, ultimately, all alone:

> Till finally you hear how
> words are coming to an

---

24 But as well as the Dantes and Joyces of high literature, Beckett also enjoyed reading *Sherlock Holmes* mysteries, Len Deighton thrillers, Robert Louis Stevenson, and French thrillers.

end. With every inane word a little nearer to the last. And how the fable too. The fable of one with you in the dark. The fable of one fabling of one with you in the dark. And how better in the end labour lost and silence. And you as you always were. Alone. (52)

It sounds all nice and neat, this ending with the word 'alone'. But it is not true. No human is ever alone. No one is 'alone'. Even when someone has lived in a wilderness for seventy years, they are still not 'alone', they are still fully encultured, still full up of socialization, still full of other people. Even when people live alone they are surrounded by millions of people. All the people who influenced them, and all the people with whom they've come into contact, in all manner of means, are all there inside them. Everyone is full up with everyone else. If you read or write or speak or get involved in any kind of communication (or if you're alive at all), you are immediately encultured,

immediately socialized. Beckett's dream of being absolutely alone is an understandable but over-simplified one. For Beckett should know, being a 'French writer', living in France, and being surrounded by French culture, that the process of enculturation is crucial, and unavoidable. Everybody is socialized, in all manner of ways. French writers, such as Simone de Beauvoir, Hélène Cixous, Jacques Lacan, Julia Kristeva, Jacques Derrida and all the cultural theorists and deconstructionists and post-structuralists have all emphasized the importance of culture in the forming of a person. It is culture, not nature, that forms women, says de Beauvoir.[25]

So Samuel Beckett's nice and simple ending of *Company*, that one ends up 'alone' is a pretence. For there are always voices in the dark, there are always narrators writing and editing one's life, there are always mediations, transformations, enculturations, socializations,

25 *Marie-Claire*, October 1976, in E. Marks, 1981, 152

initiations and revisions
going on. Although one
seems to be alone, one
always has people teeming
around inside. Although one
seems to be alone, one
always has people reading
and writing and speaking
inside oneself, in one's many
selves. Although one may
seem to be alone, one always
has company.

3

In the Zone of Stones

Ill Seen Ill Said

Ill Seen Ill Said is a text that comments upon itself as it is being written. The narrator questions his creativity as he employs it in phrase after phrase. The notions of imagination, creation, artistic endeavour, fiction, narrativity and meaning are continually questioned throughout the work. The book is, first of all, 'ill seen' or 'mal vu'. That is, it is not seen fully or properly by the author/ narrator. The subject – the woman in the zone of stones - is weakly or not fully imagined or conceived. She is 'ill seen' by her creator, the author. Further, the text is 'ill said' or 'mal dit'. That is, it is an unfinished, incomplete, distorted text and expression.

All of Samuel Beckett's texts may be described as 'ill said'.For Beckett always emphasizes the incompleteness and limitations of language. If only he could say things purely, in a form of total communication. But words are limited and limiting, so all his fictions and writings are 'ill said'. In this work, the very subject itself - the woman and the stones and the life lived there - is 'ill seen'. The author is not sure about what he is seeing, in his imagination, much as the old woman's own experience is 'ill seen'. Then, to compound this problem, the expressing of what is 'ill seen' is 'ill said'.

Ill Seen Ill Said is a text that writes itself and questions itself simultaneously. The authorial commentary may be seen in a traditional text as being intrusive. Such authorial notations, such as '[o]n' or '[g]ently gently', destroy the diegetic effect and authority of the text. Instead, *Ill Seen Ill Said* is supremely a meta-text, a series of Chinese boxes of texts in which the upper layer of self-questioning is as crucial as the deeper layers dealing with death, emotions, nostalgia and a poignant sense of lyricism.

Ill Seen Ill said is full of the usual Beckettian obsessions: with black/ white light/ dark imagery, with presence/ absence, with past/ present, with wilderness, with cycles and seasons, with death and decay, with stillness and motion, etc. *Ill Seen Ill Said,* like *Company,* is self-consciously a resumé of every Beckettian preoccup-ation, and with all former

Beckettian texts, from the early novels, *Mercier and Camier, More Pricks Than Kicks, Watt*, etc, through the plays, *Godot, Endgame, Happy Days*, etc, to the prose pieces of the 1960s and 70s. You can use the *Nohow* trilogy as a way in to all of Beckett's former works. The is a summing-up piece, simultaneously compressing and reducing earlier works and remaking them entire in a new form of poetry and poetics where the 'missaid' is finally triumphant. In the late 1980-83 trilogy, Beckett's 'literature of the unword' has its apotheosis. As *Worstward Ho* puts it:

> Said is missaid. Whenever said said said missaid. From now said alone. No more from now now said and now missaid. From now said alone. Said for missaid. For be missaid. (36-37)

The text of *Ill Seen Ill Said* opens with a powerful evocation of the old woman and her celestial experiences. The opening is distinctly poetic, almost a resumé of the fundamental poetic experience, which is of an enlarged, expanded, mythic and spiritual sense of being-in-the-world.

She sees Venus rise: she is indulging in simple nature mysticism. Already, in the first of the sixty one paragraphs, Beckett is evoking a sense of religious feeling, timelessness, cyclical movement and time, the heavens, and the ubiquitous atmospheric twilight, the scene of poetry since time immemorial, but very distinctly a part of modern poetry from the Romantics such as Heinrich Heine in his *North Sea* cycle, or Charles Baudelaire in his *Flowers of Evil*, with all those Parisian twilights:

> From where she lies she sees Venus rise. On. From where she lies when the skies are clear she sees Venus rise followed by the sun. Then she rails at the source of all life. On. At evening when the skies are clear she savours its star's revenge. At the other window. Rigid upright on her old chair she watches for the radiant one. Her old deal spindle-backed kitchen chair. It emerges from out the last rays and sinking ever brighter is engulfed in its turn. On. She sits on erect and rigid in the deepening gloom. (7)

As critics have noted, the language of *Ill Seen Ill Said* is self-consciously lyrical, with its evocations of Romantic and Symbolist poetic styles, from Charles Baudelaire through Paul Verlaine and Stéphane Mallarmé to Paul Valéry.[26]

The poetry of *Ill Seen Ill Said* is at once Samuel Beckett's most self-consciously contrived and his most deeply poetic. Clearly, underneath the stylish poesie and the postmodern self-reflexivity, there is a deep well of feeling in this text. Once you pierce the membrane of word magic, you find the usual Beckettian preoccupations of yearning and loss, of death and

---

26 Marjorie Perloff: "Between verse and prose: Beckett and the new poetry", *Critical Inquiry*, (9), no 2, December 1982, 415-433; Monique Nagem: "Know Happiness: Irony in *Ill Seen Ill Said*", in R. Davies, ed, 78f

contact, of solitude and despair.

Many things are familiar: the chair, from *Still*, and the old woman sitting in the chair, like the woman in *Rockaby*. The upland wilderness is familiar, too, from *The Trilogy* or one of the four novellas.

Absence is presence in the art of Samuel Beckett. The woman flits in out of sight, in and out of the texts, in and out of meaning, yet she is definitely there. Her absence is sometimes more acute than her presence. The elements of her environment point towards her, even when she is not there: the buttonhook, the window, the building, the chair, the pallet. In her absence, the old woman is a powerful presence.

The woman comes into being in a fragmented way, for she is so definitely and self-consciously a literary construct. How much better it would be if she and the whole thing were 'pure figment' the narrator ponders. 'If only all could be pure figment', he says (20).

But of course, this is precisely what the text is. Fiction is all figment. But the longing for all to be 'pure figment' stems from something deeper than an artistic possibility. It stems from a desire for all of life to be all figment, for Beckett in this text more forcefully than in many other texts aches for the simplicity of total oblivion. Often he recalled the lecture he attended when C.G. Jung spoke of a girl who thought she had never really been born. Beckett wondered it would be like to never have been born at all. That would be the true void, the true oblivion.

Of a passage in *Footfalls*, Beckett wrote that the mother 'was going to say: "…the same where she was *born*". But that is wrong. She just began. "It began. There is a difference. She was never born.'[27] He felt, and this anxiety is clearly manifested in his texts, that he too had not been born properly. Something of him was left in the womb, perhaps, some spiritual or ontological chunk of himself. The desire to

---

27 In W. Asmus, 1977, 84

expire in the void, then, can be seen as the old Freudian desire for *regressus ad uterum*, the old Freudian longing of the male for total dissipation in the larger Female – the Goddess – otherwise known as a desire to 'return to the womb'.

The trouble is, the narrator of *Ill Seen Ill Said* acknowledges, that confusions inevitably appear once you start writing fiction, or any kind of writing:

> Already all confusion. Things and imaginings. As of always. Confusion amounting to nothing. Despite precautions. If only she could be pure figment. Unalloyed. (21)

The trouble is that Samuel Beckett cannot stand ambiguity even while he loves to cultivate it. So, if he writes a simple word such as 'morning', he has to go and explain which morning it was, and what sort of morning, and how the morning relates to whoever is in the fiction. It can't be just *any* morning. Yet, also, it *can* be just any morning.

As Pozzo cries in *Waiting For Godot*, one day you were born, one day you'll die, what does it matter what day it was? Yet Beckett must be precise. He must know everything, even if he doesn't put all this precision into his texts.

Hence we find the obsession with measurements, with numbers and mathematics, with getting descriptions of things absolutely right. We see this happening all the time in Beckett's narration. First some statement is made, then a voice, like the devil cackling into one's ear, pipes up and says, no, it's not like that, get it right, it was like this. So every statement is qualified, and followed by a counter-statement. Thus, in the extract from *Text For Nothing* XI, the narrator continually adjusts what is being stated, as if, in split brain psychology, the left hemisphere sets in order what the left hemisphere wants or imagines. This push-me-pull-you is found in Western art in figures such as God and the Devil, or

49

Francesco Petrarch and his interrogator St Augustine in his *Secretum*,[28] or good and evil, or Laurel and Hardy, whom Beckett enjoyed:

> And it's still the same old road I'm trudging, up yes and down no, towards one yet to be named, so that he may leave me in peace, be in peace, be no more, have never been. Name, no, nothing is nameable, tell, no, nothing can be told, what then, I don't know, I shouldn't have begun. (Prose, 107)

Samuel Beckett's narrators want to be absolutely sure of something, so they remain eternally hesitant and unsure, because they acknowledge the uncertainty and ambiguity of knowing for certain. Words such as 'truth' or 'purity' or 'honesty' are never used in Beckett's texts without irony – or vehemence.

So Samuel Beckett uses the technique of poetic negativity, stating always what something *isn't* to get at what it *is*. Is-ness in Beckett's art is a product of *isn't-ness*, so to speak. That is, Beckett's way of approaching the target or essence is through absence, silence, the spaces between words and negativity.

He says 'the slightest eloquence becomes unbearable'.[29] Clearly, Samuel Beckett detests hyperbole, superlatives, any form of poetic over-indulgence. Yet *Ill Seen Ill Said*, in terms of its own poetic world, is often wordy and over-indulgent. Beckett's style goes for musical repetition, and repetitiousness is supremely over-indulgent, stylistically. Repeating the same words and phrases over and over, isn't that supremely indulgent? Texts such as *Lessness* and *For to End Yet Again* repeat the same phrases in slightly different ways, as if being spewed out in mathematically-altered forms by a computer. Beckett often writes as if he's writing-by-numbers, that is, as if he has written out some

---

28 In Francesco Petrarch's *Secretum*, see Morris Bishop: *Petrarch and His World*, Chatto & Windus, 1964, 204-7

29 Quoted in L. Harvey, 1970, 249

numerical sequence, a geometric or Fibionacci sequence, perhaps, and is repeating his phrases according to arithmetic methods.

In terms of its own severely reduced vocabulary and syntax, Beckett's new poetry can be very eloquent. He hates eloquence, yet how eloquent *Ill Seen Ill Said* is, really, with its beautiful evocations of twilight and star-gazing.

Samuel Beckett's is a poetry of *absence* – absence of text a well as absence of character. Thus, the old woman in *Ill Seen Ill Said* fades in and out of view. She is there but not there. She may be dead, like the mother in *Footfalls*, whose voice we hear but who is almost certainly already dead.[30] The narrator cannot decide which he prefers – oblivion or creation, absence or presence. To create creates problems, but oblivion is to give up, to submit to not 'going on'. So he goes on with his enterprise of the creation of a text, even while he has grave reservations about it. At every step forward, the narrator wishes to demolish his edifice:

> not possible any longer except as figment. Not endurable. Nothing for it but to close the eye for good and see her. Her and the rest. Close it for good and all and see her to death. (30)

Ill Seen Ill Said is full of these sighs of despair and these spurs into action, these cries of giving up hope and relentlessly 'going on'.

I am reminded on 'non-duality' or 'liberation', an increasingly popular spiritual view or philosophy, which posits that everything is oneness expressing itself, but there is no self here, no here, no now, and no people to think or speak about it. 'Paradise is now' in non-dualism, but people don't exist. There is only liberation, only oneness, only

---

30 See R. Thomas Simone: ""Faint but by no means invisible": a commentary on Beckett's *Footfalls*", *Modern Drama* (26, no. 4), 1983, 435-446; Karen L. Laughlin: "Seeing is perceiving: Beckett's Later Plays and the Theory of Audience Response", in R. Davies, 25f

something happening. As my friend Richard Sylvester put it:

What a wonderful relief it is to see that there is no choice, no person, no separation. Nothing you have ever done has ever led to anythng because you have never done anything. No one has ever done anything although it appears that things have been done.31

In Beckett's poetry of absence, complete oblivion is a terrifying prospect. Although the narrator of the *Nohow* trilogy employs negativity and absence, he does not wish to reduce himself and everything else to nothingness. No, nothingness, however much desired by the Beckettian protagonist or narrator, is, finally, rejected. By the tips of their worn-down fingers, Beckett's people hang on to presence and the present. At the end of the day (it's always the 'end of the day' in Beckett's texts), presence is kept, and absence is rejected.

---

31 R. Sylvester, *I Hope You Die Soon*, Non-Duality Press, 2006, 23.

The dream of total oblivion is superseded by the reality of presence, of being there instead of never having been there. For although some of Beckett's people have 'never been born', they are firmly in-the-world, they are flesh-and-blood, even while they are 'pure figment'. They are alive and in-the-world, so they have to get on with living.

The question in *Ill Seen Ill Said* is raised: what if one is 'pure figment', a character in a meta-fiction: can one still be driven to 'go on', to keep surviving? The answer is ambiguous, but the narrator seems to fall down on the side of *yes*, one must, even when one is a vague and shadowy character or non-character in a (meta)fiction, one must still 'go on'. As the narrator puts it towards the end: '[a]bsence supreme good and yet.' (58) In other words, absence is the Holy Grail, the desired end, for, surely, there will be no problems of any kind in a state of pure absence, in the Buddhist *nirvana* or the Christian nothingness of

Meister Eckhart.

Although Samuel Beckett, like Mister Eckhart, loves to 'sink down from nothingness to nothingness', as Eckhart did,[32] he was never as certain as the mystics of total dedication to the cause. That is, Beckett was never, finally, as extreme as those mystics in Christianity, Buddhism or Islam, who profess total commitment to god, to the *via negativa* of mysticism, to faith and to the mystical way.

Beckett always keeps something back. There is always that little thinking ego of René Descartes, that mind thinking over things. There is a great desire for oblivion, but it is never carried out to its logical end. As the narrator explains in *Ill Seen Ill Said*: '[a]bsence supreme good *and yet*' (my italics). Beckett retains the possibility of a possibility of something happening. Even when things are at their most desperately awful, he still retains that little seed of hope. Hope! A blasphemous word in Beckett's mythopœia, yet it is

there, underneath the seemingly relentless barrage of irony and distance and endurance.

At the end of *Ill Seen Ill Said*, it's the narrator that is tired and wants to finish the text/ story/ book, but life has not finished with the narrator. Life is always waking the narrator up again. He cannot sleep forever, though he might wish to. No. The energy of life is always waking him up, and forcing him to 'go on'. So he goes on.

This is the way with all of Beckett's texts and narrators. They yearn so much for a total finish, for an ending rather like a guillotine coming down. The head of the body of words is chopped off; the brain ceases thinking; and, with the death of the mind, with its Cartesian subject restlessly thinking and being, there is oblivion. But no. No blade comes down to slice off the text neatly and completely. There is no complete ending in Beckett's *œuvre*. His texts end ambiguously, in confusion. Even that ending

---

32 Eckhart, sermon, in F.C. Happold, 274

of *Ill Seen Ill Said* – '[n]ot
another crumb of carrion
left' (59) – is not complete,
for the narrator adds '[n]o.
One moment more. One last'
(59). There is always that
'one moment more' in
Beckett's mythos.

4

Sometimes In the Light of the Moon

Magic and Ritual in *Ill Seen Ill Said*

There is much magic, religion, astrology, occultism and ritual in *Ill Seen Ill Said*, only it is buried deep in the text. There is a surface emphasis on Venus, the moon, stars, the heavens, the sky and the 'zone of stones' which is something of a stone circle, but these motifs are pointers to a deeper layer of magic and religion which has been present in all of Sam Beckett's works.

The book itself opens with a star-gazing ritual, where the old woman sees Venus rise (7). Very soon the landscape of the book is established: the white stones, the circle, the cabin and the celestial orbits. It is a mysterious world, quite unlike any of Beckett's other spaces. Clearly, it looks back to the Irish uplands of *Molloy*, where those derelicts crawled across the wilderness. But this is an enigmatic, deeply lyrical landscape, quite spectral and otherworldly. In the second paragraph the magical rituals are elaborated, as is the exact topography of the circle:

> Chalkstones of striking effect in the light of the moon. Let it be in opposition when the skies are clear. Quick then still under the spell of Venus quick to the other

window to see the other marvel rise. How whiter and whiter as it climbs it whitens more and more the stones. (9)

The woman communes with the planets and the heavens. There is some deep mystery at work here, never defined clearly, always shifting as the narrator veers between desire and repulsion, between fictive construction and ontological deconstruction, between, in effect, being and non-being, writing and un-writing or not-writing.

The woman seems to be in a state of perpetual mourning, like the characters in *Footfalls* and *Rockaby*. She is drawn to one of the stones and communes with it. The stone is a religious object, a mirror which reflects the old woman's spiritual stillness and stasis. The woman stands still before the stone, and the stone reflects back her immobility. The woman herself is like one of the ancient stones. Only she moves. But her movement is hazy, vague, indistinct. This

vagueness reflects the narrator's own indecision. Does he really want a mobile, flesh-and-blood person in his text? He is not sure. So the woman fades in and out of view, in and out of darkness, in and out of semantic clarity. Take this passage:

> There was a time when she did not appear in the zone of stones. A long time... but little by little she began to appear. In the zone of stones. First darkly. Then more and more plain. Till in detail she could be seen crossing the threshold both ways and closing the door behind her. Then a time when within her walls she did not appear. A long time. But little by little she began to appear. Within her walls. Darkly. (13)

The woman weaves in and out view because the narrator/ author is not sure about her. Clearly, someone does not really appear darkly then 'more and more plain'. She's either there or she's not. *Ill Seen Ill Said* is a product of that process Beckett termed 'imagination dead imagine', that is, the process which questions every aspect of the creative act, from imagination to presentation, from idea to text, from inkling to reading. This uncertainty and shifting sense of beingness occurs in Beckett's last works, such as *Stirrings Still* (1988):

> As when he disappeared only to reappear later at another place. Then disappeared again only to reappear again later at another place again. So again and again disappeared again only to reappear at another place again... Disappear and reappear at another place. Disappear again and reappear again at another place again... Rise and go in the same place as ever. Disappear and reappear in another where never. Nothing to show not another where never. (Story, 117-9)

Seen but not seen, spoken but not spoken, heard but not heard. Samuel Beckett's ontological/ artistic shape-shifting occurs right up to his last work, *What is the Word*, in which the narrator or voice admits it is folly to have to 'seem to glimpse' or to 'need to seem to glimpse':

> see –
> glimpse – seem to glimpse
> –
> need to seem to glimpse –
> folly for to need to seem
> to glimpse –
> what –
> what is the word –
> and where –
> folly for to need to seem
> to glimpse what where –
> (Story, 132-3)

To seem to glimpse is to acknowledge the importance of seeing. One cannot help looking, and everywhere in Beckett's fictions we find an emphasis on Lacanian vision, on Lacanian desire and lack, and the erotic nature of looking at the obscure object of desire. These notions of seeing, the eye, desire, lack, eroticism and œdipal conflict appear throughout Beckett's work. One can read him entirely in Lacanian terms, just as one can read him entirely in terms of Jungian psychology, of in terms of French deconstruction, or in terms of linguistics, etc.

The narrator, in *Ill Seen Ill Said*, as in *Stirrings Still*, which has many similarities with the *Nohow* trilogy, wishes the woman to be pure figment, but she can't be, not wholly, for she is *already* pure figment. *Ill Seen Ill Said* shows how figments work within figments, how fictions arise from inside fictions. For fictions write themselves – every novelist knows this, that the book 'writes itself' in part. Thus, we see Beckett's woman appearing and creating a life for herself, even while the author/narrator questions this process. Does he want a character at all? Beckett (or his narrator) cannot escape creating characters. He tries to reduce his texts to merely words, without references to people or personalities. But he can't expunge the human figure, like a painter reluctant to go wholly abstract.

Even in *Worstward Ho*, the most severe of the already severe *Nohow* trilogy, humanity appears in amongst the compressed language. We hear of hands, heads, eyes, feet, boots, bones, and so on. The body is still present, as are the human emotions and human frailties. In *The Unnamable* we saw Beckett reducing his speaking self to a pair of eyes and a mouth, those two things alone assure total humanity. Even when he reduces humanity to a spotlit Mouth on a black stage, as in *Not I*, he still engages sensual human feeling, for that mouth, as commentators noted, was very human, sexual, horrible, animal, etc.[33] Mouth is indeed the Hell hole, the gateway to Hell, as the early Christian fathers, such as Tertullian (3rd century A.D.), said of women.

That feverish, desperate, self-hating sensibility is not found in the *Nohow* trilogy, which is elegiac and tranquil by comparison with some of Beckett's earlier tirades (in *Malone Dies* or *Mercier and Camier*, for example, where Beckett's vulgarity is

---

[33] See R. Thomas Simone, in R. Davies, 58; Hersh Zeifman, 1976, 35-46; Keir Elam: "*Not I*: Beckett's Mouth and the Ars(e) Rhetorica", in Enoch Brater, 1986; Katherine Kelly, 1980, 73-80

unbridled).

In *Ill Seen Ill Said* the subtext or under-themes of rituals, religion, stone circles, astronomy and magic is not intrusive, not 'obvious', not crude, as it might be. Samuel Beckett's love of time and the measurement of time is embodied in that stone circle, with its twelve sentinels or stones. In *Company* we had a consciousness looking at a watch, looking at how the second hand moves and casts a shadow (47f). In *Ill Seen Ill Said*, the space of the text is a gigantic clock, a flat circle of a clockface on the landscape, with the woman as the consciousness that activates its movement.

Ill Seen Ill Said is a text that explores the mysteries of time and space, connecting them with the time and space of the narrator/ author, so that there are a number of levels of time: the author's, the narrator's, the old woman, her past, her imagined past, the past of the ancient stones, the time of the rites that were enacted there, etc. Each time zone is symbolized in the 'zone of stones', for that stone circle, that flattened ring on the landscape, is very clearly an image of life itself, of time and space within the universe. That stone circle is the world, the sphere of the world, and the concrete manifestation of the music of the celestial spheres.

One recalls the wonderful British land artist Richard Long, who creates circles on hills and moors with rocks, or snow, or with mud on the walls of galleries, or by stamping down grass in circles. Richard Long's art makes a connection with the Earth that aims to be sacred, to bring the sacred back into the profane world.[34] With the sacred coming in, mythic time supersedes profane time, as Mircea Eliade notes.[35]

The significance of the circle is discussed at length in many places – in C.G. Jung's concept of the *mandala*, in the symbolic circle, which

---

34 See R.H. Fuchs: *Richard Long*, Thames & Hudson 1986, 43f

35 See M. Eliade, 1958

signifies infinity, eternity, cycles, etc, in stone circles such as Avebury in Wiltshire and Boscawen-Ûn in Cornwall in the U.K., in the magic circle of the magician. The creation of the magic circle in traditional Western magic is interesting, for it has a ritual aspect, as well as a mathematically precise aspect, which Beckett's characters enjoy. The magic circle is drawn nine feet in diameter with a knife or sword; it is consecrated with incantations; it has names of power written on it at special places, and so on.36

Samuel Beckett's stone circle is clearly a sacred space, with distinct boundaries, which separates sacred from profane space. That stone circle is a mythic space, a centre of the world or an *imago mundi*, as Mircea Eliade calls it37 Beckett may be ambiguous about the sacred, for he is clearly an areligious person

himself, that is, a sceptic, an unbeliever in God, for God and Christ are always dealt with sarcastically, ironically or humorously in his works (remember the jokes about crucifixion in *Waiting For Godot*, for instance). But the 'zone of stones' in *Ill Seen Ill Said* is clearly magical. Mircea Eliade explains how a space can become sacred:

> How does any space transform itself into sacred space? Simply because a sacrality is manifested there. The answer may seem to us too elementary, almost infantile. It is in effect quite difficult to understand. Since a manifestation of the Sacred, a hierophany, bears for the conscious-ness of archaic peoples a rupture in the homo-geneity of space. In more familiar terms, we would say that the manifestation of the Sacred in any space whatsoever implies for one who believes in the authenticity of this hierophany the presence of transcendent reality... The Sacred is that something altogether other to the profane. Consequently, it does not

---

36 See Richard Cavendish: *The Magical Arts: Western Occultism and Occultists*, Arkana 1984, 236f; E.M. Butler; *Ritual Magic*, Noonday Press, New York 1959

37 Mircea Eliade, 1988

belong to the profane world, it comes from somewhere else, it transcends this world. It is for this reason that the Sacred *is* the real *par excellence*. A manifestation of the Sacred is always a revelation of *being*.[38]

This sounds too grand, too pompous for Beckett's book, but it applies directly, for Beckett's work contains miniature revelations, little but often exquisite revelations which are actually religious in their intensity, although the author would deny the religious dimension. The revelations of light in *Company*, for instance, that is religious. Or the consciousness at the window staring at the dying sun in *Still*, that is religious. Or the 'zone of stones', with the twelve sentinels or presences, that is clearly a sacred space. In their own way, even though they are dejected, disgruntled, depressed and desperate, Beckett's people do have little religious experiences.

They don't interpret them as such, but they are spiritual nevertheless. This is not a new occurrence in Beckett's *œuvre*, this mystical twilight. In the twelfth *Text For Nothing*, the narrator writes in a way fully in tune with the poetic world of the *Nohow* trilogy:

A winter night, without moon or stars, but light, he sees his body, all the front, part of the front, what makes them light, this impossible night, this impossible body, it's me in him remembering, remembering the true night, dreaming of the night without morning, and how will he manage tomorrow, to endure tomorrow, the dawning, then the day, the same as he managed yesterday, to endure yesterday. (Prose, 111)

In *Ill Seen Ill Said*, the religious dimension is positively and lucidly pointed up by the narrator. Even as he goes back and forth, continually modulating and shifting his emphasis and his statements, he keeps on with his sense of magic, as in

---

38 M. Eliade, 1985, 107

paragraph 9:

But quick seize her where she is best to be seized. In the pastures far from shelter. She crosses the zone of stones and is there. Clearer and clearer as she goes. Quick seeing she goes out less and less. And so to say only in winter. Winter in her winter haunts she wanders. Far from shelter. Head bowed she makes her slow wavering way across the snow. It is evening. Yet again. On the snow her long shadow keeps her company. The others are there. All about. The twelve. Afar. Still or receding. She raises her eyes and sees one. Turns away and sees another. Again she stops dead. Now the moment or never. (15)

The act of walking, as anyone who has walked alone or in a group knows, is a ritual act. Walking can be an act of re-instating the sacred.[39] Many Beckett protagonists walk in a determined or ritualizing manner. There is May in *Footfalls* who paces up and down. Beckett is reported in saying that the 'walking up and down is the central image… [it is] the basic conception of the play'.[40] There are the many walks in *Molloy* and *Malone Dies*. There is the restlessness of *Waiting For Godot*, and the obsession with feet and boots.[41] In the *Nohow* trilogy, there is much walking, from the memories of the self, when he slipped out to his hollow in the gorse, or set out across the snow, to the pair in *Worstward Ho*, who plod on doggedly.

Walking is like writing: step by step one proceeds, much as in writing one writes word after word. Each step takes one on a journey; ditto writing. And both acts are self-hypnotic. Walking soothes the mind, and frees up the mind for dreaming. Ditto writing. Writing is a waking dream, like walking. And writers often use walking to shake up their thoughts. If they have a problem with a

40 Quoted in Walter Asmus, op.cit., 84

41 Katherine H. Burkman, 1984

text, they might for a walk. It does help. Not always. But often it does. Some of the thoughts of the artist Richard Long on walking throw light on Beckett's preoccupation with rhythm and walking:

> A walk expresses space and freedom and the knowledge of it can live in the imagination of anyone, and that is another space too. A walk is just one more layer, a mark, laid upon the thousands of other layers of human and geographic history on the surface of the land... A walk traces the surface of the land, it follows an idea, it follows the day and the night.

Richard Long's rituals of picking up stones then setting them down a few miles down a track, or picking up stones and piling them up, or of walking in circles in a wilderness – a walk which is later marked on a map, and the map becomes the 'record' of the walk – all these rituals have connotations with Beckett's characters' rituals. How similar is the old woman's walking and praying in *Ill*

Seen Ill Said with some of Richard Long's ritualized acts of art.

Richard Long talks of walking activating the sense of being-in-the-world, of bringing to awareness the passing of day and night, of time and space. This is what happens throughout Beckett's work, this making acute the sense of time and space, of emotion and death. Beckett brings the central mysteries of the human condition alive, which is what artists do. In his works, the awareness of light/ dark, life/ death, day/ night, presence/ absence is renewed. The primal mysteries are re-manifested, as in this passage from *Ill Seen Ill Said*:

> Dim the light of day from them were day again to dawn. Without on the other hand some pro-gress. Toward unbroken night. Universal stone. Day no sooner risen fallen. Scrapped all the ill seen ill said. The eye has changed. And its scribe. Absence has changed them. Not enough. Time to go again. (51)

There is presence, then, a moment later, there is absence. The woman was there, look again, she's gone. This presence/ absence encapsulates the whole of the mystery of existence with which Samuel Beckett grapples. The moment – then the moment gone. The woman – then not the woman.

The late 1980-83 trilogy is packed with explorations of an ultimate, paradoxical mystery – death. The woman is suddenly gone. There may be 'one moment more', but she is gone. Death in Beckett's work is not being there, not speaking, or not being seen, the 'glimpse' of *What is the Word*.

In *Ill Seen Ill Said* we find an acceptance of death not found in the earlier works. In *The Trilogy* and *Waiting For Godot* the characters kicked against death frenetically. Death was the biggest prick to kick against. But in the late trilogy we find a lyrical, elegiac resignation and acceptance. But it is not the acceptance of the end of *King Lear,* which

is won at such a great cost. No, Beckett's acceptance is not *Lear*-like, it is more Buddhist or Taoist, melancholy but empowering.

Presence/ absence, presence/ absence – it's almost a *mantra* in Samuel Beckett's works. You can hear his characters saying it with every step they take. Left foot: *presence*, right foot: *absence*. Step-by-step they walk, or rock, or think, thesis then antithesis, statement then counter-statement, word following word. This rhythm of duality powers all of Beckett's works. We see it in the tit-for-tat exchanges of Didi and Gogo, or in the disgruntled arguments between Krapp and his former selves.

Beckettian rhythm is a pulse, the rhythm of music, of the feet, of the heartbeat. Thus, in *Rockaby*, the rocking motion hints at the baby being rocked in the mother's arms, heartbeats, blood pulses, music, sex, and the rocking motion people use when they need comforting.

Billie Whitelaw often talks

about the way Samuel Beckett would beat out the rhythms of the speech in his plays,[42] where the pauses are as crucial as the words themselves. Whitelaw had to deliver utterly precise vocal rhythms. Beckett would speak of quarter-length pauses, and half-length pauses, as well as full-length pauses. Those gaps between words, as in Harold Pinter's drama, are crucial in Beckett's art. Rhythm has always been a key element of Beckett's poetics – look at the end of *The Unnamable*, which reaches a fevered, dithyrambic and Dionysian verbal rhythm.

Rhythm is crucial. It keeps the writer/ narrator going. Yet there is an underlying philosophical and psychological and ontological stillness or stasis in the late trilogy, and in most of Beckett's works. His characters walk and shamble about, but they don't get anywhere. They walk in circles. They only rarely get beyond their present state.

Side by side, or, rather, below, Beckettian walking there is Beckettian sitting, standing or lying. The fundamental posture in *Company* is not walking but lying down. In *Worstward Ho* the two people plod but the text revolves around a still point of self-questioning. While Beckett's characters plod on, the narrator remains motionless, watching them come and go, as he watches the old woman in *Ill Seen Ill Said* come and go. Everything in Beckett's texts ultimately refers and reverts to the narrator, the all-seeing eye, the eternal observer, the self-seeing self who narrates the text.

Thus, in *Ill Seen Ill Said* there is an underlying ontological stasis which is the point of equilibrium achieved at the end, when the text comes to a stop and something of a standstill. These are the moments of bliss, when the text seems to stop and the narrator 'breathes the void', as he puts it in the penultimate sentence:

---

42 See Billie Whitelaw in J. Calder, 1986, 83f

Endless evening. She lit aslant by the last rays. They make no difference. None to the black of the cloth. None to the white hair. It too dead still. In the still air. Voidlike calm as always. Evening and night. (29)

Who is this female presence in *Ill Seen Ill Said?* She is clearly a Goddess figure, someone who presides over a company of twelve adherents or followers, the stones or presences, who 'take' or control her as much as she controls them. It is the woman that sets the text in motion, that sets the emotional and psychological reverberations of the text in motion. Without the woman there is a lack of human presence which Beckett cannot sustain for long. We know he puts the human dimension into his texts even when, like *Worstward Ho*, the conventional elements of fiction are reduced to nothing.

She may be nameless and her personality may be vague, but the old woman is definitely a Goddess. She has affinities with the Great Goddesses of the ancient world – with Ishtar of Babylon, Isis, Kali of India and Nut or Night of Egypt. The Goddess Isis, in Apuleius' tale, says: 'I am Nature, the Mother of All/ Mistress of the elements,/ Sovereign of the Spirit/ Queen of the Dead,/ Queen of the immortals'.[43] Beckett is not as hyperbolic as Apuleius, clearly, but the same themes are here – the idea that the woman or Goddess crystallizes the mysteries of life, of death and love and time. Somehow, Beckett's old woman brings together the mysteries of life and death and time in her person. She remains a shadowy figure to the end, but she embodies ontological exploration.

Venus is mentioned in the first sentence, but it should be noted that the planet Venus, as evening star, is also sacred to Jesus and Lucifer.

43 Apuleius: *Metamorphoses*, quoted by Kathleen Alexander-Berghorn: "Isis: The Goddess of Healing", in Shirley Nicholson, ed: *The Goddess Re-awakening: The Feminine Principle Today*, Theosophical Publishing House, Wheaton, Illinois, 1989, 91

Rather than being another incarnation of the old woman, Venus in *Ill Seen Ill Said* is more like her consort, much as the Goddesses of old had their consorts (Ishtar had Tammuz, Isis had Osiris, etc).[44] As Angela B. Moorjani notes, the world of *Ill Seen Ill Said* is that of a Goddess: the pastoral elements with the cows (Goddesses are often symbolized by cows), the stone circle, the moon, etc. 'She is foremost a *mater dolorosa*,' writes Moorjani:

> the mother sorrowing for her lost lover and child (here recalling the divine shepherd Tammuz) during the desolate seasons of the year. As a *mater dolorosa*, she evokes Mary, the mother of Christ, to whose sacrifice this as most Beckettian texts makes direct reference, and with which Beckett associates

his own birth.[45]

The mother figure, often depicted as a wise crone, appears more and more in Samuel Beckett's work, so that by the time of the trilogy of late plays, *Not I, Footfalls* and *Rockaby*, she dominates the texts. Whether this mother figure relates to Beckett's own mother is a matter for biographers and gossipers. What is clear that she is yearned for and resented simultaneously. She is both loved and hated, for she is powerful. They are women, however, always seen through males eyes, through the mediations of patriarchy. The themes of *Rockaby*, for instance, are feminine mysteries seen from a male viewpoint – the patriarchal viewpoint is made explicit by the violence of the language:

> saying to the rocker
> rock her off
> stop her eyes
> fuck life
> stop her eyes

44 See Marija Gimbutas: *the Language of the Goddess*, Thames 7 Hudson 1989; Monica Sjoo & Barbara Mor: *The Great Cosmic Mother*, Harper & Row, San Francisco 1987

45 Angela B. Moorjani: "The *Magna Mater* Myth in Beckett's Fiction: Subtext and Subversion", in Friedman, 153-4

rock her off
rock her off
(Works, 442)

In *Footfalls, Rockaby* and
Ill Seen Ill Said we have
women centre stage but with
great voids in their lives.
Each piece depicts great loss
and emptiness. It's all over,
and these women are ghosts
of their former selves - if
they were former selves at
all. The central image of the
dramatic trilogies - Mouth
hovering in darkness, May
pacing into darkness, the
woman in *Rockaby* rocking
into darkness - conveys
Beckett's message more than
the words. As Martin Esslin
writes:

> it is quite impossible to
> make sense of the words,
> what remains is a pure
> image, the poetical
> metaphor concretised
> into a picture, a moving
> and sounding picture, but
> essentially a picture
> nevertheless.[46]

---

46 Martin Esslin: "Visions of
Absence: Beckett's *Footfalls, Ghost
Trio*, and *...but the clouds...*,", in
Ian Donaldson, ed: *Transformations
in Modern European Drama*,
Humanist Press, Atlantic Highlands,
1983, 121-2

The old woman is clearly
the Goddess in her death
aspect. The feminine and
death are firmly entwined in
Ill Seen Ill Said, as in so
much of male/ patriarchal
literature. The old woman
and death also means the
death of the old woman
herself, which symbolizes for
the narrator the death of the
whole creative enterprise of
writing:

> not possible any longer
> except as figment. Not
> endurable. Nothing for it
> but to close the eye for
> good and see her. Her and
> the rest. Close it for good
> and all and see her to
> death. Unremittent. In the
> shack. Over the stones. In
> the pastures. The haze. At
> the tomb. And back. And
> the rest. For good and all.
> To death. Be shut of it all.
> (30)

In Robert Graves' Goddess
mythology, the Goddess is a
Triple Goddess, of youth,
motherhood and old age,
variously symbolized in
Spring, Summer and Winter,
or the New, Full and Old
moons, or in birth, growth

and death, etc.[47] Beckett's old woman is a Death-Goddess, of the old, waning moon, associated with the Goddesses of witchcraft: Hecate, Diana, Circe and Persephone, those Goddesses that preside over the mysteries of death and rebirth. Beckett emphasizes the seasons and the cycle of life in his text, as James Joyce did throughout *Ulysses*. Beckett's old woman is at the end of the cycle – indeed, many of Beckett's characters are derelicts, always at the end of something. Some, like the Unnamable, cling on to the old regime. But the old woman is resigned to it; she is not feverish, like Mouth in *Not I*, or Hamm in *Endgame*.

The images of *Ill Seen Ill Said* back up this notion of the old woman as a Goddess of Death: the sacrifical lamb, the flowers, the stones, and the chalk-white stones, so strangely lit by the moon (the moon is *the* symbol and emblem of all Goddesses,

and embodies the cycles of life, death and renewal as it grows and wanes). This image of the chalk and stones has connotations with all manner of sepulchres and tombs, prehistoric tumuli and barrows. The old woman does not live in a tomb, however, but a stone ring, which some see as ancient forms of astronomical observatories, while others see them as sites of celebration, where the eternal mysteries of birth, love and death were ritualized.[48]

Late Samuel Beckett fiction often prefers old women as the embodiment for him of the human condition. Women have for millennia presided over the mysteries of birth, life and death. For neo-Jungians (we

47 Robert Graves: *The White Goddess*, Faber 1961; Jeremy Mark Robinson, *Blinded By Her Light: The Love-Poetry of Robert Graves*, Crescent Moon, 1991

48 See books by Aubrey Burl and Gerald Hawkins for the classic descriptions of stone circles as astronomical sites; on the wackier interpretations of stone rings, see Michael Dames: *The Avebury Cycle*, Thames & Hudson 1977, Paul Devereux: *Symbolic Landscapes: The Dreamtime Earth and Avebury's Open Secrets*, Gothic Image, Glastonbury, Somerset 1992, and Tom Graves: *Needles of Stone, Revisited*, Gothic Image, Glastonbury 1986

have seen that Beckett tends more towards Carl Jung than Sigmund Freud), 'woman' is Goddess as the whole of time and space, the whole of the created universe. Neo-Jungians such as Erich Neumann see the Goddess as the 'Great Round', the whole of the cosmos.[49] Joseph Campbell writes:

> The female represents what in Kantian termin-ology we call the *forms of sensibility*. She is time and space itself, and the mystery beyond her is beyond all pairs of opposites... *everything* is within her... Everything you can think of, every-thing you can see, is a production of the Goddess.[50]

Other neo-Jungians see the Goddess as the Eternal Mother of Johann Wolfgang von Goethe's *Faust*, the *prima materia* of alchemy, the chaos from which all is created, as well as the vile stepmother of fairy tales and the dualistic mother/ witch of infant psychology.[51]

In her indispensable book on symbolism, another neo-Jungian, J.C. Cooper lists some of the symbols of 'woman' and the mother figure:

> The woman is symbolized by all that is lunar, receptive, protective, nourishing, passive, hollow or to be entered, sinuous, cavernous, diamond- or oval-shaped; the cave, walled garden, well, door, gate, cup, furrow, sheath, shield; also anything connected with the waters, the ship, shell, fish, pearl. The crescent moon, the reflected light of the moon, and the star are pre-eminently her attributes. (194)

Disregarding the sexism in this list of attributes, we find many of them in Beckett's work: the passive, meditative stance, the shelters such as caves and huts, the

---

49 Erich Neumann: *The Great Mother*, Bollingen/ Princeton University Press 1972

50 Joseph Campbell: *The Power of Myth*, 167

51 See Johannes Fabricus: *Alchemy*, Aquarian Press, 1989, 50f; Marie-Louise von Franz: *The Feminine in Fairy Tales*, Spring Publications, Dallas, Texas, 1972;

motifs of doors, windows
and openings, the sea, the
moon and the star.

5

No Words Left

Worstward Ho

Worstward Ho is the most severe of Sam Beckett's texts, but it is not the most difficult to read by any means. *How It Is* is without doubt the most dense and difficult of Beckett's texts, for it's a long work. In the short pieces, such as *Lessness* or *Ping*, one can manage concentrated, close readings, but with *How It Is*, it is difficult to sustain the intense reading that the text demands. *Worstward Ho* is quite short – it is 47 pages in the Calder (U.K.) edition, but this is because it is printed, like the other two in the 1980-83 trilogy, in 16 point size type.

Worstward Ho is not a tricky text. In fact, it is a joy to read – especially to read aloud, like Will Shakespeare or Mark Twain. Beckett has reduced his vocabulary even further than he did in *Company* and *Ill Seen Ill Said*, and those texts were themselves compressed. Yet *Worstward Ho*, like some of the short fizzles and texts of the 1960s and 70s, such as *Still* or *Imagination Dead Imagine*, is deeply poetic. Name any of the 'great' poetic texts – Rainer Maria Rilke's *Duino Elegies*, Dante Alighieri's *Vita Nuova*, or Maurice Scève's *Délie* – and Beckett's *Worstward Ho* is as poetic, as beautiful and melancholy and lucid.

Worstward Ho is another installment in Beckettian reductionism, that urge to squeeze out of art all the unnecessary baggage. Brian Finney remarks of *Worstward Ho*: there is a

> new brevity, a frontal assault on the traditional language of prose... Beckett sets out to destroy normal syntax and narrative continuity in the hope of creating a new language out of which the form of being can at least be constructed.[52]

Samuel Beckett's compression and reductionism is rather like that of the sculptor Constantin Brancusi, who aimed to reduce his sculptures to the essence or Platonic idea of the form of his subject, whether a bird, fish, head, torso or kiss.[53] Brancusi's drive towards getting at the 'essence of things' is similar to Beckett's, and both artists stress the importance of form – but not outer, surface form, but inner, spiritual form. Beckett is not interested in surfaces, as he explained in his his book on *Proust* (64). Beckett has said that his idea of form, which he explained to Harold Pinter, was someone screaming with pain in a hospital. That noise, he says, is the kind of form he was looking for.[54]

Worstward Ho is different from most fictions, for even more than *Company* or *Ill Seen Ill Said*, *Worstward Ho* is a work that comments rigorously on itself as it creates itself. The pleasure of Beckett's texts is precisely the gaps between what is expected in fiction and what Beckett delivers. As Judith E.

---

[52] Brian Finney, in J. Ascheson, 76

[53] 'What is real is the not the external form, but the essence of things', said Brancusi, in the catalogue of a 1926 exhibition at the Brummer Gallery in New York. See also: Eric Shanes: *Constantin Brancusi*, Abbeville Press, New York 1992, 7f

[54] Quoted in Deirdre Bair

Dearlove comments, his works:

> never proffer completed conventional structures, his pieces depend on the reader's perception of the disparity between the recognizable fragments he is given and the tradition they deliberately do not fulfil.[55]

Samuel Beckett has long subverted tradition and expectations. Each of his fictions, from the earliest ones, subvert, parody, spoof and play with genres, expectations, traditions and conventions. Beckett loves upturning traditional fictive processes.

Thus, in *Company*, he says all right, let there be a story, and as he goes along he stops, thinks, then admits it would be good for the person to have a voice, and so on. Each addition flies in the face of the traditional novel, which has a complex set of rules governing character, plot, theme, diegesis and narrativity. In *Ill Seen Ill Said* the narrator

urges himself onward with phrases such as 'on' or 'gently'. Beckett's early works – *Murphy, Mercier and Camier, Watt* – systematically spoofed the novel, while *The Trilogy* took this parodic tendency to extremes. The *Nohow* trilogy is no different, for it ruthlessly sends up the whole novelistic and artistic enterprise.

Beckett's texts are not mere strings of words, any words, written randomly. No. His words make sense. Further, they tell stories. He cannot stop himself from telling stories. Similarly, he has to have a character, and even in his most ruthlessly reduced texts, there is a human character, and scenes, and some kind of narrative. In *Worstward Ho*, which at first glance is a exploration of form purely, with no 'meaning' or 'story', in fact has images and scenes – a woman on her knees in a graveyard (45), two people plodding along (15f) and so on.

Worstward Ho is created out of Beckett's eternal obsession to express himself,

---

55 Judith E. Dearlove 1982, 39-40

to say something, and yet having nothing to say, nothing with which to say, no means to say, and a hatred of saying. Yet he says, he says things, he writes.

He creates a new poetry to deal with this negation of language. He tags on endings such as 'less' and 'most' to amplify his vocabulary, even as he reduces it to its minimum, the '[m]eremost minimum' (9). The new poetry consists of words such as 'beyondless', 'missaid', 'so-said', 'unworsenable' and ''unlessable' (11, 20, 24, 42, 43).

As an example of Samuel Beckett's new poetry, here is a passage from *Worstward Ho* which expresses the eternal tension in Beckett's art between speaking and not speaking, between presence and absence, and between life and death:

> Longing the so-said mind long lost to longing. The so-missaid. So far so-missaid. Dint of long longing lost to longing. Long vain longing. And longing still. Faintly longing still. Faintly vainly longing still. For fainter still. For faintest. Faintly vainly longing for the least of longing. Unlessenable least of longing. Unstillable vain least of longing still. Longing that all go. Dim go. Void go. Longing go. Vain longing that vain longing go. Said is missaid. Whenever said said said missaid. From now said alone. No more from now now said and now missaid. From now said alone. Said for missaid. For be missaid. (36-37)

All of Beckett's artistic and philosophic concerns are summarized in *Worstward Ho*, and many of them are found in this extract. Beckett's philosophy is a system of negations, and here he pinpoints the desire to negate desire, the desire to transcend desire or, as he puts it, he is 'faintly vainly longing for the least of longing' (36). He longs, in other words, for the end of longing. Now, though, in *Worstward Ho*, the fervour has gone, to be replaced by a quietness, a gentleness of resignation.

His aim is never to make a

fool of himself in prose. Beckett's literature is a 'literature of the unword', as he called it, a poetics which must never allow over-romantic or even mildly romantic writing. His mode of expression is based on a 'syntax of weakness', as he called it.56 Beckett detests gushing, foamy, lyrical, 'poetic' writing, and *Worstward Ho* aims to negate all such tendencies. As Enoch Brater comments:

> *Worstward Ho* attempts to scuttle such literary adventurism as romanticism of the worst sort, a 'Wordsworthy' opportunism that makes language the slave of sloppy sentimentality.57

Part of Samuel Beckett's reductionism and anti-silliness in prose stems from his severe editing of language and syntax, at its most extreme in *Worstward Ho*. We might re-edit or annotate the section of *Worstward Ho*

56 Quoted in Lawrence Harvey, 249

57 Enoch Brater: "Voyelles, Cromlechs and the Special (W)rites of *Worstward Ho*", in J. Ascheson, 171

quoted above like this:

[The] Longing [for] the so-said [the 'once said thus'] mind [that was] long lost to longing. The so-missaid [i.e., the very 'missaid' was mistakenly spoken]. So far [it has been] so-missaid. [By] Dint of long longing [which has been] lost to longing. [There is or has been a] Long vain longing. And [there is] longing still [despite everything]. [I am, or there is (a)] Faintly longing still. [(The)] Faintly [,] vainly longing still. [Which is longing] For fainter still. For faintest [type of 'longing still'}. [There is a] Faintly [,] vainly longing for the least of longing. [There is (a)] Unlessenable least [lessness, perhaps] of longing. Unstillable vain least [smallest part] of [the/ my] longing still. [I am/ there is (a)] Longing that all [longing, stillness, void, you name it] go [disappear]. [That the] Dim go. [And that the] Void go. [And even that the] Longing go. [There is (a)] Vain longing that vain longing [will] go. [The] Said is missaid ['mis-spoken']. [It happens] Whenever [the] said [which was/ is] said

said missaid. From now [it will be] said alone. [There will be] No more from now [that is] now said and [also] now missaid. From now [it will be] said alone. [It will be] Said for missaid. For [it'll] be missaid. (36-7)

Such a (re-)editing of a Beckett (or any) text shows how crucial is the precise order of words, the choice of words, the chaining together of words, the punctuation (no commas in the *Nohow* trilogy, for instance), the 'personal voice' (beloved of humanist criticism), all of which rewriting or editing destroys.

Desire is never wholly negated in Sam Beckett's texts, for there is always the fact of the text itself to be accounted for. Although Beckett's narrators speak of a desire to stop speaking, there is the text itself, speaking, always speaking. Thus, the artwork itself is an expression of desire, coming out of desire, even if, as in Beckett's work, the artwork dwells obsessively on the negation of desire. As the

eighth *Text For Nothing* has it:

> Only the words break the silence, all to her sounds have ceased. If I were silent I'd hear nothing. But if I were silent the other sounds would start again, those to which the words have made me deaf, or which have really ceased. But I am silent, it sometimes happens, no, never, not one second... I'll be silence, I'll know I'm silence, no, in the silence you can't know, I'll never know anything. (Prose, 96-7)

The book begins with that most hopeful and positive of Beckettian words, 'on', which is used, as usually, with lashings of irony and scorn. Yet, the text goes 'on', and as it unravels, all the usual Beckettian concerns are here; the black/ white imagery, the boots and greatcoat and hat, the shingle, decay and death, being and non-being, eyes, skulls, the void, desire, melancholy, etc.

The text begins positively, and ends with the same word, 'on'. The opening paragraph runs:

78

On. Say on. Be said on.
Somehow on. Till nohow
on. Said nohow on. (7)

The text then goes on to
demonstrate how to go on
when there can be no way
('nohow') of going 'on'.

Artistic considerations are
primary for, as with André
Gide, art and philosophy,
æsthetics and ethics, are the
same thing. Good art means
good philosophy, and vice
versa. Thus, æsthetic success
parallels success in life.
Hence Beckett's pre-
occupations in the opening
sequences of *Worstward Ho*
which have to do with
success and failure, but
modulated by a heavy sense
of irony and self-conscious
meditations on the
possibilities of art:

Nothing else ever. Ever
tried. Ever failed. No
matter. Try again. Fail
again. Fail better... The
body again. Where none.
The place again. Where
none. Try again. Fail
again. Better again. Or
better worse. Fail worse
again. Still worse again.
(7-8)

Knowing the impossibility
of ever getting it right, of ever
succeeding, the narrator
postulates the idea of 'failing
better'. Better to 'fail better'
than to 'fail worse', he
reckons. Beckett has been
'failing better' throughout his
artistic career, and here in his
last major work he shows
how to make 'failing better' a
religion, an art form.

Knowing that introducing
'characters' – he calls them
'bodies' here – is fraught with
problems, the narrator
imagines no body. But that is
no good either. There must
be a place too, but the
narrator wonders about
having no place at all. That,
too, is no good. There must
be a place. There is always,
says Beckett, the Descartes
ego thinking. If there is
always a mind thinking, there
must be a body. If there is a
body, it must be in a place.
This is the meaning of the
above extract, where the
narrator juggles with the
mechanisms of narration and
wonders if he should
dispense with them
completely. Beckett has
always been wary of adding

things. As he says: '[a]dd –.
Add? Never.' (WHo, 23), and
in *Ill Seen Ill Said* he is
always saying 'careful' to
himself: '[i]f only all could
be pure figment. Neither be
nor been nor be any shift to
be. Gently gently. On.
Careful.' (20)

    Worstward Ho is a text
that deliberately and self-
reflexively travels '[f]rom
bad to worsen', as the
narrator terms it (23). It's hell
to be 'so-said', but it's hell
too to be 'so-missaid'. To be
'missaid', though, is surely
worse than to be 'so-said'
however bad the 'so-said; is.

6

From Void To Void

Beckett and Philosophy

Worstward Ho contains a renewed fascination with the void. What void? The 'dim' void, as Samuel Beckett insists on calling it (WHo, 11). No void can be 'dim', a void is simply a void, a total, utter oblivion. As the Buddhists say of *nirvana*, it is 'made of nothing at all.'[58]

The 'void' in Beckett's work is essentially another term for that space of darkness, negation and utter realism (which some interpret as pessimism or hopelessness). Beckett has a poetic space in his texts compounded of silences, hesitations, meaningless gestures, nostalgia and desire. Beckett's void is another form of the 'wild zone', the space beyond language, the darkness that surrounds the bonfire of ordinary consciousness, as Ursula Brangwen put it in *The Rainbow*. Robert Lax writes:

> It is down there in deep sleep that Beckett lives, and where all of us live, but few in our time have been so expert in visiting that region, in staying there and bringing back a

---

58 Nagasena, quoted in John Ferguson, 1976, 133

living report.[59]

In *Worstward Ho*, the void is evoked and negated simultaneously. It is hated and desired, just as everything is in Beckett's mythopœia, from sex to landscapes to companionship to self-expression. The 'void' in *Worstward Ho* is that 'boundless bounded', '[t]henceless there. Thitherless there. Thenceless thitherless there', '[t]he dim. The void', '[s]hade-ridden void', '[u]nmoreable unlessable unworsenable evermost almost void' (11, 12, 14, 25, 42-43).

This is the void-space that is Samuel Beckett's psychic/ metaphysical interior in his works, the 'within'. As Beckett says, 'expression of the within can only be from the within'.[60] The deep irony is that Beckett's dimmest void can only occur in

writing. It is a feeling-space, certainly, experienced by individuals. But it only as a 'dim void' in the 'dim void' of language, in the spaces that writing can suggest or delineate. For, however much he is a mystic or a philosopher, Beckett always remains, first and foremost, a *writer*. Always in Beckett's writing we come back to words, to what words can do, and, just as importantly, what they can't do. As *Worstward Ho* says:

> Worsening words whose unknown. Whence unknown. At all costs unknown. Now for to say as worst they may only they only they. Dim void shades all they. Nothing save what they say. Somehow say. Nothing save they. What they say. Whosoever whence-soever say. As worst they may fail worse to say.(29)

If in Beckett's work the gaps, silences or hesitations of prose are important, these gaps, silences and hesitations are, ultimately, self-referential. The experience they point towards is just as

59 Robert Lax, letter to Nicholas Zurbrugg, 16.9.1984, quoted in Nicholas Zurbrugg: *"Ill Seen Ill Said* and the Sense of an Ending", in Ascheson, 151

60 Beckett, letter to Aidan Higgins, 22 April 1958, in *The Review of Contemporary Fiction*, 3, Spring 1983, 157

much, if not more, the experience of writing, of a text, of a reader's relation with a text. That is, the final leap in Beckett's fictions is not towards some Buddhist practice of meditation, towards some actual contemplative experience of the Tibetan Clear Light of the Void, or a life led in a Catholic monastery. No, Beckett is an *artist*, not a mystic. He does not *actually* renounce writing, although his characters try. He might advocate a philosophy of silence, but he can't keep quiet himself, and neither can his characters. His texts, too, are very loquacious. They babble. They prattle. Even the most reductive of texts, *Worstward Ho* or *Lessness*, babbles incessantly. *Worstward Ho* is a 47-page babble, a monologue or soliloquy all about the 'silence' of some abstract 'dim void'.

Beckett's texts are not manuals of mystical meditation. They are meta-texts, texts *about* meditation and darkness and silence. Further, they try to *embody*

darkness and silence in their very syntax and structure, as well as in their vocabulary. They are texts designed to *be* the darkness and silence and void. Yet, with their elaborate structures, syntax, vocabulary, design and ornate poetics, Beckett's texts never get beyond being texts or meta-texts. There is always some cut-off point in Beckett's art, a point beyond which he will not go. Beckett's texts are products of someone who denigrates production of any kind. They are creations of someone who *all the time* advocates the idiocy of creation. It's all a waste of time, Beckett's texts say. What is the 'it' here? It is the 'it all' of *Footfalls*. *When will you be through resolving/ revolving it all?* is the question that *Footfalls* asks. The answer is *never*. Never will Beckett's texts finish revolving 'it all'. Never will the texts wind up at some point of harmony and desirelessness, the Buddhist *nirvana*. Always, Beckett's meta-texts go on. As *Worstward Ho*, the text that seems to 'write' itself as it is written says:

> So leastward on. So long
> as dim still. Dim
> undimmed. Or dimmed
> to dimmer still. To
> dimmost dim. Least-most
> in dimmost dim. Utmost
> dim. Leastmost in utmost
> dim. Unworsenable
> dim.(33)

Aching for the absolute or ultimate, Samuel Beckett's metatexts fall short of it, continually. It – 'the end' – is never reached. Never.

If life is completely negated, it is simultaneously completely affirmed. The negation confirms the affirmation. The act of speaking confirms the affirmation. Even though texts such as *Imagination Dead Imagine* begins by despising and doing away with the world, yet the very act of expression, of self-negation and world-negation, ends by being self and world affirmation, the exaltation of life:

> No trace anywhere of life, you say, pah, no difficulty there, imagination not dead yet, yes, dead, good, imagination dead imagine. Islands, waters, azure, verdure, one glimpse and vanished, endlessly, omit... Go back out, move back, the little fabric vanishes, ascend, it vanishes, all white in the whiteness, descend, go back in. Emptiness, silence, heat, whiteness, wait, the light goes down, all grows dark together, ground, wall, vault, bodies, say twenty seconds, all the greys, the light goes out, all vanishes. (Prose, 145)

Even as Samuel Beckett's meta-texts crumble and decay in darkness, they persist, somehow they 'go on'. Even as there is nothing to say and nothing to do, there is every-thing to say and everything to do. The mysteries that Beckett persistently returns to – the mystery of being, of being there and then of not being there, of life and death – are fully explored in the late *Company* trilogy. These mysteries are best summed up in that enigmatic appearance/ disappearance of the old woman. The old woman can be any of us: 'she [we] can be gone at any

time.' (*III*, 17) Here, in the
presence/ absence
dichotomy, Beckett touches
on a central, perplexing and
eternally-recurring mystery of
being alive:

> She is vanishing. With the
> rest. The already ill seen
> bedimmed and ill seen
> again annulled. The mind
> betrays the treacherous
> eyes and the treacherous
> word their treacheries.
> Haze sole certitude. The
> same that reigns beyond
> the pastures. It gains them
> already. It will gain the
> zone of stones. Then the
> dwelling through all its
> chinks. The eye will close
> in vain. To see but haze.
> Not even. Be itself but
> haze. How can it ever be
> said? Quick how ever ill
> said before it submerges
> all. Light. In one treach-
> erous word. Dazzling
> haze. Light in its might at
> last. Where no more to be
> seen. To be said. Gently
> gently. (48)

Illustrations

Images on the following pages of the incomparable Billie
Whitelaw in Samuel Beckett's plays, which have close links
with the late trilogy.

Above, Whitelaw in Footfalls (© John Haynes)

Billie Whitelaw in Rockaby.

The themes of Rockaby are feminine mysteries seen from a male viewpoint –
the patriarchal view is made explicit by the violence of the language:

> saying to the rocker
> rock her off
> stop her eyes
> fuck life
> stop her eyes
> rock her off
> rock her off
> (Works, 442)

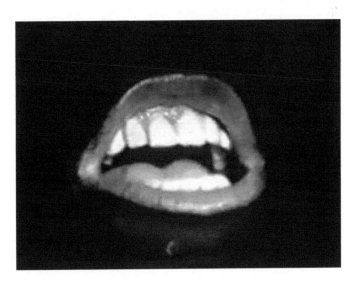

In Footfalls, Rockaby and Ill Seen Ill Said we have women centre stage but with great voids in their lives. Each piece depicts great loss and emptiness. It's all over, and these women are ghosts of their former selves – if they were former selves at all. The central image of the dramatic trilogies – Mouth hovering in darkness, May pacing into darkness, the woman in Rockaby rocking into darkness – conveys Beckett's message more than the words.

Billie Whitelaw in Happy Days
(© John Haynes)

Billie Whitelaw in Happy Days (1978)
(© BBC)

Samuel Beckett and Billie Whitelaw at work

Beatrice Manley in Rockaby,
Los Angeles, 1982 (photo by R. Goldengay)

Bibliographies

All books are published in London, England, unless otherwise stated.
Abbreviations appear after each entry

Samuel Beckett

Collected Shorter Prose 1945-1980, Calder 1984   [Prose]
Collected Poems: 1930-1978, Calder 1984   [Poems]
The Complete Dramatic Works, Faber 1990   [Works]
Waiting For Godot, Faber 1965   [WG]
Disjecta: Miscellaneous Writings, ed. Ruby Cohn, Calder 1983 [D]
The Beckett Trilogy: Molloy, Malone Dies, The Unnamable, Picador 1979
    [T]
Mercier and Camier, Picador 1988   [MC]
Murphy, Picador 1973   [Mur]
The Expelled and Other Novellas, Penguin 1988   [E]
How It Is, Calder 1964   [How]
More Pricks Than Kicks, Calder & Boyars 1970   [Kicks]
Watt, Calder 1976   W]
Proust and Three Dialogues, Calder & Boyars 1970   [Proust]
Company, Calder 1980   [C]
Ill Seen Ill Said, Calder 1982   [Ill]
Worstward Ho, Calder 1983   [WHo]
Nohow On, Calder 1992   [No]
As the Story Was Told, Calder 1990   [Story]
Compaignie, Editions de Minuit, Paris 1980
Têtes-Mortes, Editions de Minuit, Paris 1967
For to End Yet Again, Calder 1976
A Samuel Beckett Reader, ed. John Calder, Pan 1983
Happy Days: The Production Notebook of Samuel Beckett, ed. James
    Knowlton, Faber 1983
Stirrings Still, Calder, 1988
Dream of Fair to Middling Women, ed. by Eoin O'Brien & Edith Fournier,
    Black Cat Press, Dublin. 1992
Eleuthéria, Minuit, Paris, 1995
Samuel Beckett: The Complete Short Prose, 1929-1989, ed., intr. S. E.
    Gontarski, Grove, New York, 1995

Poems: 1930-1989, Calder, 2002
Samuel Beckett: The Grove Centenary Edition of Samuel Beckett, ed. by
    Paul Auster, New York: Grove Press, 2006
*Beckett Remembering, Remembering Beckett: Uncollected Interviews
    with Samuel Beckett and Memories of Those Who Knew Him*,
    Bloomsbury, 2006

Others

Robert Martin Adams: *After Joyce*, Oxford University Press, New York
    1977
D. Albright. *Beckett and Aesthetics*, Cambridge University Press, 2003
Miriam Allot, ed: *Novelists on the Novel*, Routledge 1963
James Ascheson & Kateryna Arthur, eds: *Beckett's Late Fiction and
    Drama*, Macmillan 1987
Walter Asmus: "Rehearsal notes for the German premiere of Beckett's *That
    Time* and *Footfalls* at the Schiller-Theater Werkstatt, Berlin (directed
    by Beckett)", tr. Helen Watanabe, *Journal of Beckett Studies*, (2),
    Summer 1977
A. Atik. *How it Was: A Memoir of Samuel Beckett*, Faber, 2001
Deidre Bair: *Samuel Beckett: A Biography*, Cape 1978
Helen L. Baldwin: *Samuel Beckett's Real Silence*, Pennsylvania State
    University Press, University Park 1981
Georges Bataille: *Literature and Evil*, tr. Alistair Hamilton, Calder 1973
Gregory Battock, ed: *Minimal Art: A Critical Anthology*, Studio Vista 1969
R. Begam. *Samuel Beckett and the End of Modernity*, Stanford University
    Press, Stanford, CA, 1996
Leo Bersani: *A Future For Astynanax*, Boyars 1978
Enoch Brater, ed: *Beckett at 80*, Oxford University Press, New York 1986
Katherine H. Burkman: "Initiation rites in Samuel Beckett's *Waiting for
    Godot*', *Papers in Comparative Studies*, 3, 1984
Lance St John Butler: *Samuel Beckett and the Meaning of Being*,
    Macmillan 1984
John Calder, ed: *As No Other Dare Fail: For Samuel Beckett on his 80th
    Birthday, by his friends and admirers*, Calder 1986
Joseph Campbell: *The Power of Myth*, with Bill Moyers, ed. Betty Sue
    Flowers, Doubleday, New York 1988
—. *An Open Life*, Larson Publications, New York 1988
—. *Myths To Live By*, Paladin 1985
—. *The Hero's Journey: Joseph Campbell on his Life and Work*, ed. Phil
    Cousineau, Harper & Row, San Francisco 1990
Albert Camus: *The Outsider*, tr. Stuart Gilbert, Penguin 1961
—. *A Happy Death*, tr. R.Howard, Penguin 1973

J.E.Cirlot: *A Dictionary of Symbols,* Routledge 1981

Ruby Cohn: *Just Play: Beckett's Theater*, Princeton University Press 1980

Steven Connor: *Samuel Beckett: Repetition, Theory and Text,* Blackwell 1988

J.C. Cooper: *An Illustrated Dictionary of Traditional Symbols,* Thames & Hudson 1978

A. Cronin. *Samuel Beckett: the Last Modernist*, HarperCollins, 1996

P. Davies. *Beckett and Eros: Death of Humanism*, Macmillan, 2000

Robin J. Davies & Lance St John Butler, eds: *'Make Sense Who May': Essays on Samuel Beckett's Later Works*, Colin Smythe, Gerrards Cross, Buckinghamshire, 1988

Judith E. Dearlove: *Accommodating the Chaos: Samuel Beckett's Nonrelational Art*, Duke University Press, Durham, North Carolina 1982

René Descartes: *A Discourse on Method and Selected Writings*, tr. Veitch, E. P. Dutton, New York 1951

Jonathan Dollimore & Alan Sinfield, eds: *Political Shakespeare*, Manchester University Press 1985

John Drakakis, ed; *Alternative Shakespeares*, Routledge 1988

R.P. Draper, ed: *Tragedy: Developments in Criticism: A Casebook*, Macmillan 1980

Colin Duckworth: *Angels of Darkness: Dramatic Effect in Beckett and Ionesco*, Allen & Unwin 1972

Mary Eagleton, ed: *Feminist Literary Criticism*, Longman 1991

Mircea Eliade: *Ordeal by Labyrinth*, University of Chicago Press 1984

—. *A History of Religious Ideas*, I, Collins 1979

—. *Patterns in Comparative Religion*, Sheed & Ward 1958

—. *Symbolism, the Sacred and the Arts*, Crossroad, New York 1985

—. *Myths, Dreams and Mysteries*, Harper & Row, New York 1975

Martin Esslin, ed: *Samuel Beckett: A Collection of Critical Essays,* Prentice-Hall, New Jersey 1965

John Ferguson: *An Illustrated Encyclopaedia of Mysticism,* Thames & Hudson 1976

Brian Fitch: *Beckett and Babel*, University of Toronto Press, Canada 1988

—. "The Relationship Between *Compagnie* and *Company*: One Work, Two Texts, Two Fictive Universes", in A. Friedman

G.S. Fraser: *The Modern Writer and His World*, Penguin 1964

J.G. Frazer: *The Golden Bough*, abridged edition, Macmillan 1922/ 59

Alan Friedman: *The Turn of the Novel*, Oxford University Press 1966

—. and Charles Rossman & Dina Sherzer, eds: *Beckett Translating/ Translating Beckett*, Pennsylvania State University Press, University Park 1987

Andre Gide: *The Journals of Andre Gide,* vol. II, tr. Justin O'Brien, Secker & Warburg 1948

Johann Wolfgang von Goethe: *The Sorrows of Young Werther,* tr. Michael Hulse, Penguin 1989

L. Gordon. *Reading Godot*, Yale University Press, New Haven, CT, 2002

Lawrence Graver & Raymond Federman, eds: *Samuel Beckett; The Critical Heritage*, Routledge and Kegan Paul 1979
—. eds: *Samuel Beckett: Waiting For Godot,* Cambridge University Press 1989
M. Gussow. *Conversations With and About Beckett*, Grove Press, New York, 1996
F.C. Happold, ed. *Mysticism*, Penguin 1970
J.D. O'Hara, ed: *Twentieth Century Interpretations of Molloy, Malone dies, the Unnamable: A collection of Critical Essays*, Prentice-Hall, New jersey 1970
Lawrence Harvey: *Samuel Beckett: Poet and Critic*, Princeton University Press, New Jersey 1970
Clive Hart: *Language and Structure in Beckett's Plays*, Colin Smythe, Gerrards Cross, bucks, 1986
Ronald Hayman: *Samuel Beckett*, Heinemann 1980
C.G. Jung: *Memories, Dreams, Reflections*, Collins 1967
Katherine Kelly: "The Orphic Mouth in *Not I*", *Journal of Beckett Studies,* 6, Autumn 1980, 73-80
Andrew Kennedy: *Samuel Beckett*, Cambridge University Press 1989
Hugh Kenner: *A Reader's Guide to Samuel Beckett*, Thames & Hudson 1973
—. *Samuel Beckett: A Critical Study*, Calder 1962
James Knowlson, ed: *Samuel Beckett: Krapp's Last Tape*, Brutus Books 1986
—. *Light and Darkness in the Theatre of Samuel Beckett*, Cambridge University Press 1989
—. and John Pilling, eds: *Frescoes of the Skull: The Later Prose and Drama of Samuel Beckett*, Calder 1979
—. *Damned to Fame: the Life of Samuel Beckett*, Bloomsbury, 1996
Weston La Barre: *The Ghost Dance,* Allen & Unwin 1972
—. *Muelos*, Columbia University Press, New York 1985
Jacques Lacan and the *Ecole Freudienne*: *Feminine Sexuality,* ed. Juliet Mitchell and Jacqueline Rose, Macmillan 1982
D.H. Lawrence: *A Selection from Phoenix,* ed. A.A.H. Inglis, Penguin 1971
Andrew Marissel: *Samuel Beckett*, Edition Universitaires, Paris 1963
Elaine Marks & Isabelle de Courtivron, eds: *New French Feminisms: an Anthology*, Harvester Wheatsheaf 1981
Vivain Mercer: *Beckett/ Beckett*, Oxford University Press 1979
Toril Moi: *Sexual/ Textual Politics: Feminist Literary Theory*, Methuen 1985
Fernando Molina; *Existentialism as Philosophy*, Prentice-Hall, New jersey 1962
Friedrich Nietzsche: *Beyond Good and Evil*, tr. Zimmern, Allen & Unwin 1907/ 67
—. *A Nietzsche Reader*, ed. R.J. Hollingdale, Penguin 1977
—. *A Portable Nietzsche*, ed. W. Kaufmann, Viking Press, New York 1960
Rudolf Otto: *The Idea of the Holy*, Oxford University Press 1958

Sylvia Paine: *Beckett, Nabokov, Nin: Motives and Modernism*, Kenniket Press, National University Publications, Port Washington 1981

John Pilling: *Samuel Beckett*, Routledge & Kegan Paul 1976

—. ed. *The Cambridge Companion To Beckett*, Cambridge University Press, Cambridge, 1994

—. *A Samuel Beckett Chronology*, Palgrave Macmillan, Basingstoke, 2006

Hema V. Raghavan: *Samuel Beckett: Rebels and Exiles in His Plays*, Lucas, Liverpool 1988

Alec Reid: *All I Can Manage, More Than I Could: An Approach to the Plays of Samuel Beckett*, The Domen Press, Dublin 1968

Peter Redgrove: *The Black Goddess and the Sixth Sense, Bloomsbury 1987*

Arthur Rimbaud: *Complete Works, Selected Letters*, tr. Walter Fowlie, University of Chicago Press 1966

Jeremy Mark Robinson: *Gide: Fiction and Fervour*, Crescent Moon 1992

—. *Samuel Beckett Goes Into the Silence*, Crescent Moon 1992

—. *Rimbaud: Arthur Rimbaud and the Magic of Poetry*, Crescent Moon, 1992

Bertrand Russell: *A History of Western Philosophy*, Allen & Unwin 1971

—. *Why I am Not a Christian,* Allen &Unwin 1963

—. *Bertrand Russell's Best,* Allen & Unwin 1971

Jean-Paul Sartre: *Being and Nothingness*, tr. Hazel Barnes, Methuen 1969

—. *The Psychology of Imagination*, Methuen 1972

Arthur Schopenhauer: *Essays and Aphorisms*, Penguin 1970

Edith Sewell: *The Structure of Poetry*, Routledge & Kegan Paul 1951

Elaine Showalter, ed: *The New Feminist Criticism*, Virago 1986

—. ed: *Speaking of Gender*, Routledge 1988

Ninian Smart: *The World's Religions*, Cambridge University Press 1989

W.T. Stace: *Mysticism and Philosophy*, Macmillan 1961

Valerie Topsfield: *The Humour of Samuel Beckett*, Macmillan 1988

Paul Valéry: *An Anthology*, Routledge 1977

Mary Warnock: *Existentialism*, Oxford University Press 1970

David Watson: *Paradoxical Desire in Samuel Beckett's Fiction*, Macmillan 1991

Alan Watts: *The Way of Zen,* Penguin 1962/ 80

—. *Tao: The Watercourse Way,* Cape, London, 1976

Raymond Williams: *Marxism and Literature*, Oxford University Press 1971

Ludwig Wittgenstein: *Tractatus Logico-Philosophicus,* tr. D.F. Pears & B.F. McGuiness, Routledge & Kegan Paul 1974

—. *Philosophical Investigations*, tr. G. Anscombe, Blackwell 1968

—. *On Certainty*, eds. Anscombe & Wright, Blackwell 1979

Richard Woods, ed: *Understanding Mysticism, Athlone Press 1980*

Katherine Worth: *Beckett the Shape-Changer: A Symposium*, Routledge & Kegan Paul 1975

Hersh Zeifman: "Being and non-being: Samuel Beckett's *Not I*", *Modern Drama*, 19, no.1, March 1976

ANDREI TARKOVSKY

JEREMY MARK ROBINSON

POCKET GUIDE

Andrei Tarkovsky is one of the great filmmakers of recent times.

This book covers every aspect of Tarkovsky s artistic career, and all of his output, concentrating on his seven feature films: *Ivan's Childhood, Andrei Roublyov, Solaris, Mirror, Stalker, Nostalghia* and *The Sacrifice*, made between 1962 and 1986.

Part One of this study focusses on the key elements and themes of Andrei Tarkovsky's art: spirituality; childhood; the film image; poetics; painting and the history of art; the family; eroticism; symbolism; as well as technical areas, such as script, camera, sound, music, editing, budget and production.

Part Two explores Tarkovsky's films in detail, with scene-by-scene analyses (in some cases, shot-by-shot). Tarkovsky emerges as a brilliant, difficult, complex and poetic artist.

Fully illustrated. This new edition has been revised and updated.

ISBN 19781861713957 Pbk   9781861713834 Hbk

andy goldsworthy
touching nature

WILLIAM MALPAS

Contemporary British sculptor Andy Goldsworthy makes land and
environmental art, a sensitive, intuitive response to nature, light, time,
growth, change, the seasons and the earth. Goldsworthy's sculpture is
becoming ever more popular, appearing in TV documentaries, public works,
and Holocaust memorials. Goldsworthy has exhibited around the world, and
has become one of the foremost contemporary sculptors in Great Britain.

The book has been updated and revised for this new edition.

ISBN 9781861714122 Pbk   ISBN 9781861714138 Hbk
Fully illustrated   www.crmoon.com

Thomas A. Christie

JOHN HUGHES
& EIGHTIES CINEMA
Teenage Hopes & American Dreams

John Hughes (1950-2009) is one of the best-loved figures in 1980s American filmmaking, and considered by many to be among the finest and most celebrated comedy writers of his generation. His memorable motion pictures are insightful, humanistic, culturally aware, and paint a vibrant picture of the United States in a decade of rapid social and political change.

Bibliography, notes, illustrations   372pp.
ISBN 9781861713896 Pbk   ISBN 9781861713988 Hbk
Also available: *Ferris Bueller's Day Off: Pocket Movie Guide*

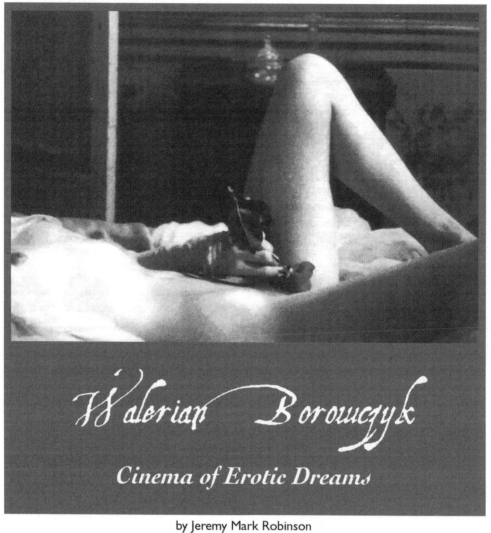

Walerian Borowczyk

Cinema of Erotic Dreams

by Jeremy Mark Robinson

Walerian Borowczyk (1923-2006) was a Polish artist, animator and filmmaker who lived in France for much of his life. He is the author of European art cinema masterpieces *Goto: Island of Love, Blanche* and *Immoral Tales*, some surreal animated shorts, and controversial films such as *The Beast*. This new book concentrates on Borowczyk's feature films, from *Goto* to *Love Rites*, which contain some of the most extraordinary images and scenes in recent cinema. Erotica for some, porn for others, Borowczyk's films are highly idiosyncratic and unforgettable.

Bibliography, notes, 110 illustrations   252pp.
ISBN 9781861713674 Pbk   ISBN 9781861713124 Hbk

Also available: *Walerian Borowczyk: The Beast: Pocket Movie Guide*

'Cosmo Woman'

The World of Women's Magazines

by Oliver Whitehorne

Fashion, image-making, sexism, gender, identity, materialism, feminism, commodity capitalism in the 'women's magazine' market. Ranging from the monthly 'glossies' (*Cosmopolitan, Marie Claire, Elle* and *Vogue*) to the 'homely' weeklies (*Bella, Best* and *Woman's Own*), through the 'style press' (*Arena, GQ, i-D, The Face*) to 'teenage' magazines (*Jackie, Smash Hits, Mizz* and *Just Seventeen*), this is one of the very few full-length analyses of the cultural products that sell in their millions.

Bibliography, illustrations, notes 168pp
ISBN 9781861712653 Hbk ISBN 9781861712851 Pbk

Life, Life
Selected Poems

Arseny Tarkovsky

translated and edited by Virginia Rounding

Arseny Tarkovsky is the neglected Russian poet, father of the acclaimed film director
Andrei Tarkovsky. This new book gathers together many of Tarkovsky's most lyrical
and heartfelt poems, in Rounding's clear, new translations. Many of Tarkovsky's poems
appeared in his son's films, such as *Mirror, Stalker, Nostalghia and The Sacrifice*.
There is an introduction by Rounding, and a bibliography of both Arseny and
Andrei Tarkovsky.

Bibliography and notes 124pp 3rd ed ISBN 9781861712660 Hbk ISBN 9781861711144

MAURICE SENDAK

& the art of children's book illustration

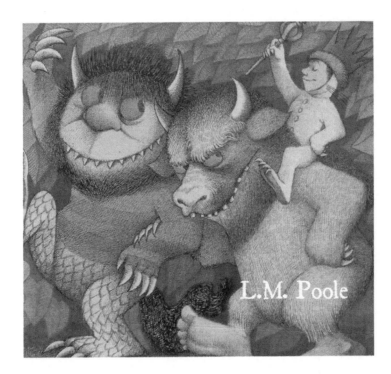

L.M. Poole

Maurice Sendak is the widely acclaimed American children's book author and illustrator. This critical study focuses on his famous trilogy, *Where the Wild Things Are*, *In the Night Kitchen* and *Outside Over There*, as well as the early works and Sendak's superb depictions of the Grimm Brothers' fairy tales in *The Juniper Tree*. L.M. Poole begins with a chapter on children's book illustration, in particular the treatment of fairy tales. Sendak's work is situated within the history of children's book illustration, and he is compared with many contemporary authors.

Fully illustrated. The book has been revised and updated for this edition.

ISBN 9781861714282 Pbk   ISBN 9781861713469 Hbk

Beauties, Beasts, and Enchantment

CLASSIC FRENCH FAIRY TALES

Translated and with an Introduction
by Jack Zipes

A collection of 36 classic French fairy tales translated by renowned writer Jack Zipes.
Cinderella, Beauty and the Beast, Sleeping Beauty and *Little Red Riding Hood* are among the classic fairy tales in this amazing book.
Includes illustrations from fairy tale collections.
Jack Zipes has written and published widely on fairy tales.

'Terrific... a succulent array of 17th and 18th century 'salon' fairy tales'
- *The New York Times Book Review*

'These tales are adventurous, thrilling in a way fairy tales are meant to be... The translation from the French is modern, happily free of archaic and hyperbolic language... a fine and sophisticated collection' - *New York Tribune*

'Enjoyable to read... a unique collection of French regional folklore' - *Library Journal*

'Charming stories accompanied by attractive pen-and-ink drawings' - *Chattanooga Times*

Introduction and illustrations   612pp.   ISBN 9781861712510 Pbk   ISBN 9781861713193 Hbk

CRESCENT MOON PUBLISHING

web: www.crmoon.com e-mail: cresmopub@yahoo.co.uk

ARTS, PAINTING, SCULPTURE

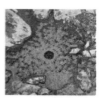

The Art of Andy Goldsworthy
Andy Goldsworthy: Touching Nature
Andy Goldsworthy in Close-Up
Andy Goldsworthy: Pocket Guide
Andy Goldsworthy In America
Land Art: A Complete Guide
The Art of Richard Long
Richard Long: Pocket Guide
Land Art In the UK
Land Art in Close-Up
Land Art In the U.S.A.
Land Art: Pocket Guide
Installation Art in Close-Up
Minimal Art and Artists In the 1960s and After
Colourfield Painting
Land Art DVD, TV documentary
Andy Goldsworthy DVD, TV documentary
The Erotic Object: Sexuality in Sculpture From Prehistory to the Present Day
Sex in Art: Pornography and Pleasure in Painting and Sculpture
Postwar Art
Sacred Gardens: The Garden in Myth, Religion and Art
Glorification: Religious Abstraction in Renaissance and 20th Century Art
Early Netherlandish Painting
Leonardo da Vinci
Piero della Francesca
Giovanni Bellini
Fra Angelico: Art and Religion in the Renaissance
Mark Rothko: The Art of Transcendence
Frank Stella: American Abstract Artist
Jasper Johns
Brice Marden
Alison Wilding: The Embrace of Sculpture
Vincent van Gogh: Visionary Landscapes
Eric Gill: Nuptials of God
Constantin Brancusi: Sculpting the Essence of Things
Max Beckmann
Caravaggio
Gustave Moreau
Egon Schiele: Sex and Death In Purple Stockings
Delizioso Fotografico Fervore: Works In Process 1
Sacro Cuore: Works In Process 2
The Light Eternal: J.M.W. Turner
The Madonna Glorified: Karen Arthurs

LITERATURE

J.R.R. Tolkien: The Books, The Films, The Whole Cultural Phenomenon
J.R.R. Tolkien: Pocket Guide
Tolkien's Heroic Quest
The *Earthsea* Books of Ursula Le Guin
Beauties, Beasts and Enchantment: Classic French Fairy Tales
German Popular Stories by the Brothers Grimm
Philip Pullman and *His Dark Materials*
Sexing Hardy: Thomas Hardy and Feminism
Thomas Hardy's *Tess of the d'Urbervilles*
Thomas Hardy's *Jude the Obscure*
Thomas Hardy: The Tragic Novels
Love and Tragedy: Thomas Hardy
The Poetry of Landscape in Hardy
Wessex Revisited: Thomas Hardy and John Cowper Powys
Wolfgang Iser: Essays and Interviews
Petrarch, Dante and the Troubadours
Maurice Sendak and the Art of Children's Book Illustration
Andrea Dworkin
Cixous, Irigaray, Kristeva: The *Jouissance* of French Feminism
Julia Kristeva: Art, Love, Melancholy, Philosophy, Semiotics and Psychoanalysis
Hélene Cixous I Love You: The *Jouissance* of Writing
Luce Irigaray: Lips, Kissing, and the Politics of Sexual Difference
Peter Redgrove: Here Comes the Flood
Peter Redgrove: Sex-Magic-Poetry-Cornwall
Lawrence Durrell: Between Love and Death, East and West
Love, Culture & Poetry: Lawrence Durrell
Cavafy: Anatomy of a Soul
German Romantic Poetry: Goethe, Novalis, Heine, Hölderlin
Feminism and Shakespeare
Shakespeare: Love, Poetry & Magic
The Passion of D.H. Lawrence
D.H. Lawrence: Symbolic Landscapes
D.H. Lawrence: Infinite Sensual Violence
Rimbaud: Arthur Rimbaud and the Magic of Poetry
The Ecstasies of John Cowper Powys
Sensualism and Mythology: The Wessex Novels of John Cowper Powys
Amorous Life: John Cowper Powys and the Manifestation of Affectivity (H.W. Fawkner)
Postmodern Powys: New Essays on John Cowper Powys (Joe Boulter)
Rethinking Powys: Critical Essays on John Cowper Powys
Paul Bowles & Bernardo Bertolucci
Rainer Maria Rilke
Joseph Conrad: *Heart of Darkness*
In the Dim Void: Samuel Beckett
Samuel Beckett Goes into the Silence
André Gide: Fiction and Fervour
Jackie Collins and the Blockbuster Novel
Blinded By Her Light: The Love-Poetry of Robert Graves
The Passion of Colours: Travels In Mediterranean Lands
Poetic Forms

POETRY

Ursula Le Guin: Walking In Cornwall
Peter Redgrove: Here Comes The Flood
Peter Redgrove: Sex-Magic-Poetry-Cornwall
Dante: Selections From the Vita Nuova
Petrarch, Dante and the Troubadours
William Shakespeare: Sonnets
William Shakespeare: Complete Poems
Blinded By Her Light: The Love-Poetry of Robert Graves
Emily Dickinson: Selected Poems
Emily Brontë: Poems
Thomas Hardy: Selected Poems
Percy Bysshe Shelley: Poems
John Keats: Selected Poems
Joh n Keats: Poems of 1820
D.H. Lawrence: Selected Poems
Edmund Spenser: Poems
Edmund Spenser: Amoretti
John Donne: Poems
Henry Vaughan: Poems
Sir Thomas Wyatt: Poems
Robert Herrick: Selected Poems
Rilke: Space, Essence and Angels in the Poetry of Rainer Maria Rilke
Rainer Maria Rilke: Selected Poems
Friedrich Hölderlin: Selected Poems
Arseny Tarkovsky: Selected Poems
Arthur Rimbaud: Selected Poems
Arthur Rimbaud: A Season in Hell
Arthur Rimbaud and the Magic of Poetry
Novalis: Hymns To the Night
German Romantic Poetry
Paul Verlaine: Selected Poems
Elizaethan Sonnet Cycles
D.J. Enright: By-Blows
Jeremy Reed: Brigitte's Blue Heart
Jeremy Reed: Claudia Schiffer's Red Shoes
Gorgeous Little Orpheus
Radiance: New Poems
Crescent Moon Book of Nature Poetry
Crescent Moon Book of Love Poetry
Crescent Moon Book of Mystical Poetry
Crescent Moon Book of Elizabethan Love Poetry
Crescent Moon Book of Metaphysical Poetry
Crescent Moon Book of Romantic Poetry
Pagan America: New American Poetry

MEDIA, CINEMA, FEMINISM and CULTURAL STUDIES

J.R.R. Tolkien: The Books, The Films, The Whole Cultural Phenomenon
J.R.R. Tolkien: Pocket Guide
The *Lord of the Rings* Movies: Pocket Guide
The Cinema of Hayao Miyazaki
Hayao Miyazaki: *Princess Mononoke*: Pocket Movie Guide
Hayao Miyazaki: *Spirited Away*: Pocket Movie Guide
Tim Burton : Hallowe'en For Hollywood
Ken Russell
Ken Russell: *Tommy*: Pocket Movie Guide
The Ghost Dance: The Origins of Religion
The Peyote Cult
Cixous, Irigaray, Kristeva: The *Jouissance* of French Feminism
Julia Kristeva: Art, Love, Melancholy, Philosophy, Semiotics and Psychoanalysis
Luce Irigaray: Lips, Kissing, and the Politics of Sexual Difference
Hélene Cixous I Love You: The *Jouissance* of Writing
Andrea Dworkin
'Cosmo Woman': The World of Women's Magazines
Women in Pop Music
HomeGround: The Kate Bush Anthology
Discovering the Goddess (Geoffrey Ashe)
The Poetry of Cinema
The Sacred Cinema of Andrei Tarkovsky
Andrei Tarkovsky: Pocket Guide
Andrei Tarkovsky: *Mirror*: Pocket Movie Guide
Andrei Tarkovsky: *The Sacrifice*: Pocket Movie Guide
Walerian Borowczyk: Cinema of Erotic Dreams
Jean-Luc Godard: The Passion of Cinema
Jean-Luc Godard: *Hail Mary*: Pocket Movie Guide
Jean-Luc Godard: *Contempt*: Pocket Movie Guide
Jean-Luc Godard: *Pierrot le Fou*: Pocket Movie Guide
John Hughes and Eighties Cinema
Ferris Bueller's Day Off: Pocket Movie Guide
Jean-Luc Godard: Pocket Guide
The Cinema of Richard Linklater
Liv Tyler: Star In Ascendance
Blade Runner and the Films of Philip K. Dick
Paul Bowles and Bernardo Bertolucci
Media Hell: Radio, TV and the Press
An Open Letter to the BBC
Detonation Britain: Nuclear War in the UK
Feminism and Shakespeare
Wild Zones: Pornography, Art and Feminism
Sex in Art: Pornography and Pleasure in Painting and Sculpture
Sexing Hardy: Thomas Hardy and Feminism

The Light Eternal is a model monograph, an exemplary job. The subject matter of the book is beautifully
organised and dead on beam. (Lawrence Durrell)
It is amazing for me to see my work treated with such passion and respect. (Andrea Dworkin)

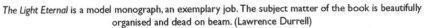
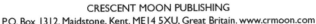

CRESCENT MOON PUBLISHING
P.O. Box 1312, Maidstone, Kent, ME14 5XU, Great Britain. www.crmoon.com

cresmopub@yahoo.co.uk   www.crescentmoon.org.uk

14591838R00068

Printed in Great Britain
by Amazon.co.uk, Ltd.,
Marston Gate.